FIASCO

DIRTY ACES MC

LANE HART

D.B. WEST

COPYRIGHT

Edited by Angela Snyder
Cover by Melissa Gill Designs

WARNING: THIS BOOK IS NOT SUITABLE FOR ANYONE UNDER 18. IT CONTAINS STRONG LANGUAGE, VIOLENCE, AND GRAPHIC SEX SCENES.

SYNOPSIS

Fiasco has always been the guy who can't do anything right. In fact, it's why he was given his unfortunate nickname.

When he takes two bullets during a shooting, Fiasco nearly loses his life. And in a way, dying may have been the easy way out.

But once he saw Joanna's face, the angelic nurse doing everything she could to save his life, he wanted nothing more than to live.

Overcoming his injuries is just the first obstacle Fiasco will have to face. If he can't get back to his construction job soon, he'll lose everything he's worked so hard to have, along with all the people who depend on him.

With Joanna's help, Fiasco begins to wonder if he could be more than the screw up of the Dirty Aces MC, right before it all comes crashing down on him yet again.

CHAPTER ONE

Phillip "Fiasco" Stafford

"*C*ome out of the woods, you stupid son of a bitch! The longer you hide, the worse it'll hurt!"

Chuck's voice is angry and slurred from drinking all day as his boots stomp through the fallen leaves in the woods behind our trailer park. He's not my father, but he acts like he is. I hate him, and I wish my mom would leave him. She's tried to kick him out, more than once, but he's like a cockroach that refuses to go away.

Rosie whines underneath me, making me realize that I was holding her muzzle too tight. "Shh," I whisper to her. If she would run away from me, I would let her go, but she's a good dog, sweet and loyal. She never leaves my side, not since I found her in the dumpster a few months ago when she was just a puppy. I can't afford to take her to the vet, but I think she may be pregnant.

Tears make my eyes blur as the sound of crunching leaves grow closer and closer to where I'm hiding inside of an old refrigerator someone threw out with the other piles of junk. I should've kept running, but I twisted my ankle and couldn't put any weight on it. Hiding was the best I could do. I was hoping it would get dark before he came after us, but I was wrong.

Chuck is right about one thing. I'm so stupid. Stupid, stupid, stupid!

I knew better than to throw the ball with Rosie in the trailer. I didn't mean for it to bust Chuck's new flat screen. He loved that damn thing more than anything. He loved it so much he'll kill me for it.

The crunching of leaves suddenly stops, and then the door to the fridge is yanked open so fast I scream like a girl.

Chuck grabs me by my hair and drags me out with Rosie clutched in my arms.

"I'm sorry! I'm so sorry!" I tell him through the sobs, glad I can't see his face when he lets go of my long hair and it falls into my eyes. "I'll buy you another one, I swear!"

"You ain't got fifty cents for lunch, much less a thousand goddamn dollars!"

"I'll get a job! Please," I say, even though we both know it would take me years to earn a thousand dollars even if someone would hire a twelve-year-old idiot.

Rosie growls at Chuck, and I rub her head to try and get her to calm down and be quiet, to let me take this punishment instead of reminding him of her.

"I'll be takin' the payback out of your hide!" Chuck roars before his fist slams down on the back of my head, making me see spots when I squeeze my eyes closed. The toe of his shoe hits my stomach and grazes Rosie's side, making her whine.

"Wait!" I beg, desperate to stop him from hurting her again. "Rosie's having puppies," I blurt out. "I'll sell them."

"Like anyone would pay a dollar for one of her stinkin' mutts!"

"I can tell people they're bulldogs, and they'll believe me," I assure him.

"I ain't gonna have no more mouths to fucking feed!" he yells. I hear the sound of a gun cocking right before the bullet explodes so close to my ears that the world goes silent. Too silent.

"NO!" I scream at the top of my lungs as my body jerks, pulling me out of the nightmare. I try to sit up, but there's a burning pain inside of me, eating through me, that stops me along with someone's hands on my shoulders. "Don't touch me! Don't fucking touch me!" I scream, and they thankfully let go. So, it wasn't my mom's old boyfriend. Nothing I said ever made him stop, so it was just that goddamn dream again…

My eyelids are heavy, but I try to open them to figure out where the hell I am. Dark hair and a concerned face are hovering over me. I finally recognize the man.

"Calm down, Fiasco," Nash says. "You're going to be okay."

The tension in my body eases up seeing my MC brother and hearing his calming voice. "Where…am…I?" I ask, wincing with each word thanks to the pain in my side and down my lower leg.

"We're, ah, at a friend's house. You were shot."

"Sh…shot?" I say. "No. His bullet didn't hit me…"

"You were shot in the side and in the leg outside the Knights of Wrath bar," Nash assures me, giving me too much information at one time. My brain feels like it's working even slower than usual as I repeat his words in my head a few times until they start to make sense.

Knights of Wrath is a familiar term. Those were the guys we were patching over. There was a party. We were all drinking and fucking… Oh yeah, I remember now. I was fucking one of their club girls from behind while she made out with another chick against the brick wall in the alley. Then a car pulled up, tires squealing. I turned my head to see who it was, not giving a shit if they watched us fuck when there was a sudden burning in my side and in my lower leg that dropped me to my knees.

"Fiasco, can you hear me?" Nash asks, his voice muffled more than before.

"Take it easy on him. I just gave him more pain meds, and they're trying to pull him under so they can do their job," a woman says before her face appears above me. She looks like a beautiful, dark-haired angel.

"I think he was having a nightmare," Nash tells her.

"The meds can put you in a deep sleep," the angel says. Then she smiles down at me warmly and says, "Sweet dreams."

My eyes close as if on command, doing exactly what she said. I hope to have sweet dreams instead of my usual nightmares. I bet I will, since she's there with me keeping the bad dreams away.

CHAPTER TWO

Joanna Patton

There's a big, muscular blond man in my bed, taking up more than half of the queen size mattress, naked other than a pair of boxer briefs.

He's the first I've slept with since my divorce, and he is much easier on the eyes than the man I was married to. Bill was fifteen years older than me, barely two inches taller than me at five foot-seven and was missing most of the brown hair that was meant to cover the crown of his head. I used to look at the thick, curly forest of hair growing from his chest and think that it must have gotten lost and detoured on its way north.

Despite his below-average looks, I thought I was in love with him when we first met. My adoptive parents had both recently died; I had just made the decision to sell the family home and farm to pay for medical bills and the funeral. I think I just wanted someone to take care of me for a little while, and that's what Bill did. At first.

But after about three months of living together as husband and wife, I quickly grew tired of him and his odd fetishes. It wasn't your normal run-of-the-mill foot fetish or even a little bondage. No, Bill got excited for...my hair. While most guys prefer oral sex, Bill usually only wanted to wrap my long, straight, dark brown hair around his dick and come in it, which was so disturbing and gross. The first time he wanted to do it, I agreed, thinking that once he had done it, he would get over the unusual urge. Instead, it only made him want to do it again and again until hair sex was the only type of sex in our marriage. No orgasms for me, thank you very much. I suggested he go to therapy or that we go to therapy as a couple. He refused, so I asked for a divorce. After a certain point of realizing he preferred my hair to the rest of me, I knew I wasn't in love with him either. He was just there when I needed someone, and I grabbed on to him.

Until now, I don't think I ever understood Bill's strange obsession. But wouldn't you know, my first thought when I was left alone with the injured biker, looking like a fallen statue of Adonis, was that he looks good enough to eat and that I wanted to run my fingers through his straight, floppy blond hair. I immediately hate myself for the inappropriate thought about a stranger, like I had crossed some horrible ethics line. Never in the four years that I've been a registered nurse have I looked at a patient and thought about them in such a lustful way.

Fiasco.

That's what Nash, Wirth and Malcolm, his so-called friends, call him. Although, to me, it sounds like an awful insult.

Sitting beside his large, muscular frame on the bed, I reach over to check his forehead and cheek for a temperature with my palm, wishing I had one of those instant, infrared thermometers. My touch causes him to stir, and then his big, hazy, brown eyes are open and looking right at me. I finally use that as an excuse to push his hair out of his eyes. It's just as soft and silky as it looks.

"You're...still...here," he says, and then the corners of his lips try and go up into a smile before he groans in pain.

"Sorry I woke you up," I whisper to him.

"Where's…everyone?" he tries to sit up and then falls right back down to the mattress.

"Nash and the guys just left. Go back to sleep…" I start to call him Fiasco like they all did, but it just sounds too cruel. "Can you tell me your name?"

"Fiasco," he answers automatically.

"No, your real one."

"Oh. It's…Phillip," he says softly.

"I'll be here, Phillip. Just sleep and give your body time to heal."

"Okay," he agrees, the word trailing off into a gentle snore as he drifts away, his consciousness turned off as quickly as a lightbulb.

OVER THE NEXT FEW HOURS, I stay by Phillip's side, dozing occasionally on my little sliver of bed, while Casey, my friend and fellow coworker, tends to Hunt, the other injured biker they left behind to heal. Hunt was incredibly lucky that a bullet just grazed the side of his head and part of his ear, or he would be a dead man.

More than once I've wanted to ask what happened, where they were and why people were shooting at them, but I kept my mouth shut. The less I know about the MC's business, the better off I probably am. Maybe I should've turned them away when the group of strange men showed up at my door. I couldn't, though; not if it meant someone dying who I could've tried to save. I'm certain they would not have wanted to show up at a hospital to have police start asking questions.

The doorbell rings late that afternoon, and I have a feeling I know who it will be. I wait and listen to see if Casey will get the door. When she doesn't, I go into the living room, surprised that neither Hunt nor Casey is in there where I left them earlier, when he was recovering on the sofa. Maybe they left without saying goodbye. There's a cup of coffee on the kitchen table, and the pillow and blanket are still draped across the sofa.

I open the door and see Nash on the other side of the glass.

"Hey." I unlock and open the storm door, then move aside for him to come in.

"Hey. Sorry to just drop in on you. How are the patients?" he asks, looking hesitant as he steps inside and glances around at the empty living room.

"I thought maybe you had heard from Hunt since he disappeared while I was with Phillip."

"Phillip?" He furrows his handsome face in confusion. There's something…familiar about him, although I'm not sure what it is. Maybe I've seen him around town before.

"Fiasco," I clarify. "He said his real name is Phillip."

"I didn't know that. How is he?"

"He's mostly sleeping, but I think he's doing okay so far. He was awake and alert long enough to tell me his name, so that's a good sign. You can come see him…"

"Sure, thanks."

I turn and start down the hallway with Nash behind me. We're about to go into the bedroom when I notice the light is on in the hall bathroom, the door shut. Then I hear soft voices coming from inside followed by a loud gasp and then what is definitely a moan.

"I think we found Hunt and Casey," Nash whispers from behind me. My cheeks go up in flames because I've never been one for casual sex or even around anyone else having sex. And the loud, noisy kind is not the type I've ever encountered in the bedroom, sad but true. I even jump when something or someone hits the bathroom door hard enough to shake it, then the sounds *really* grow louder.

"We can, ah, go on in here," I tell Nash, urging him into the bedroom ahead of me so I can close the door behind us to try and drown out the noise.

"Sorry about that," he says.

"Why are you apologizing? They're both adults," I remark.

"Yes, but that's not why I brought him here," he says.

"It's…fine."

We both pretend we don't hear the muffled grunts and groans when we move closer to the bed where Phillip is sleeping. I press my palm to his forehead, and his skin is noticeably warmer. "I think he has a fever."

"Shit," Nash says.

"I'm already giving him what antibiotics I had here, but we may need something stronger, along with more morphine."

In order to get the stronger medicines, I may have to call in a favor from a new friend in the hospital pharmacy and ask them to do something I didn't think I would ever do – steal medicine from the hospital. Thankfully, it's a small community hospital where everyone knows and trusts everyone else, even if they shouldn't. While a prescription is needed for all patients, I don't think anyone actually compares the number of prescriptions to the number of drugs that go out.

I make the call, and then Nash volunteers to go meet and pay my friend for his help.

While he's gone, Fiasco jerks in his sleep and groans as his temperature keeps climbing. I try and cool him down with a wet rag on his face, neck and chest, but it only seems to make him more uncomfortable.

"Shh, it's okay," I tell him. "I'm going to take care of you."

Talking to him seems to calm him down, so I keep at it until Nash returns, coming right to the bedroom without knocking as if he knows how urgent it is for us to get more antibiotics in his friend.

"Did you get it?" I ask, and he holds up what looks like a reusable lunch bag.

"Yes. I know how risky this is to you and your friend. Like I told him, if anything happens, I told him to say I threatened his life at gunpoint to make him steal."

"Hopefully no one will notice they're missing," I say as I take the bag from him, glad to see Thomas put some syringes in here too.

Once I get everything measured out, I push the liquid into the IV I started on Phillip and wait to see if they help.

I've just sat back down on the empty side of the bed when Casey comes into the room. Her auburn hair is pulled up in a messy bun like mine, although much messier after sex. She's practically glowing, face flushed like a heavy coat of blush has been applied perfectly. The blissed out look on her face falls just a little when she sees Nash standing there. "Oh, sorry. I would've knocked if I knew you had company."

"It's okay," we both say.

"I need to slip outside to call and give Malcolm an update," Nash says when he pulls out his phone. As soon as he leaves the room, Casey closes the door behind him. Not only is her hair disheveled, but her scrub top is on inside out.

"What's up?" I ask, trying not to blush since it wasn't me who was having sex with a strange man in someone else's bathroom and it's none of my business what she does. We're both single, recently divorced women free to do what we want.

"I was just going to see if you need anything," Casey says. "After Hunt gets a quick shower, I'm going to give him a ride to the Dirty Aces' pool hall."

"Sounded like you already gave him a ride," I comment, unable to help myself. "And he shouldn't get the side of his head wet."

"I know. That's what I told him when I was…helping him get undressed," she says, biting down hard on her bottom lip. "Oh, hell, I don't care if you think less of me! He's feeling much better after a little…sexual healing."

"Sexual healing. Right," I reply with a roll of my eyes.

"Hunt was feeling down about the shooting happening on his watch and getting his ear messed up…" she trails off.

"And you just helped lift him up."

"Exactly," she says with a big grin, not sounding the least bit embarrassed.

"You should give it a try." Casey nods her head toward the unconscious man in bed.

"He's burning up with a fever. Thankfully, Thomas was able to sneak some meds out. Now we just have to wait and hope he can fight it off."

"He looks tough enough to fight off anything," Casey says as she goes over to his side of the bed to get a better look at him.

"Infection can take down anyone."

"True," she agrees. When she reaches down to feel his forehead, I feel an unusual rush of jealousy, which is incredibly stupid since I barely know the man. "He's warm but not too hot, maybe a hundred degrees?"

"Well, it needs to come down," I snap at her, and she quickly pulls her hand away from him.

"Calm down, Joanna. I'm not the one who shot the man twice," Casey huffs.

"I know," I say with a sigh. "It's just…this is all sorts of crazy, these guys coming out of nowhere and now we're trying to save his life. Do you know that they call him Fiasco?"

"Fiasco?" she repeats with her brow furrowed. "Like he's a fuck up?"

"Even if he is, that's incredibly cruel."

"Yeah, it is," she agrees with a frown. "He could kick all of their asses if he wanted, but he doesn't. They're his friends, so he must be okay with the name."

"Maybe," I agree as I climb into bed and run my fingers down his arm to check his pulse. The small touch causes goosebumps to raise all the way down, which is odd.

"Pulse strong?"

"Stronger than it was since I gave him some blood."

"I still can't believe you did that," Casey says.

"I've had all the tests before I got hired a few weeks ago. My blood is clean."

"Yes, but it's just…you really do go the extra mile for patients."

"If it can save their life, yeah."

Fiasco, Phillip, moans and then rolls on his side toward me. His eyes flutter open a second before he's out again.

"Talking to him seems to help," I say as I brush his hair back out of his eyes again.

"Touching him would probably help even more," Casey encourages.

"I can't touch a man I don't know like that. He's a patient."

"It doesn't have to be dirty!" she exclaims. "Skin-to-skin contact is good for everyone. It's a proven fact."

"If you say so," I tell her with a smile and a shake of my head as I think about the skin-to-skin contact she just had with Hunt in my bathroom.

"I will not apologize for having amazing sex with a hot biker," she says with her shoulders back to push her ample chest out.

"I didn't say anything!" I remind her. "You can have amazing sex with whoever you want."

"So can you," she says with a waggle of her brows as she starts to the door.

"Want me to bring you something to eat when I come back?"

"Sure, thanks," I tell her since I don't want to leave Phillip's side even to make something to eat.

CHAPTER THREE

Joanna

I t's been almost twenty-four hours since I gave Phillip the pain meds and started the antibiotics, but he still hasn't woken up. I'm well beyond concerned at this point. I've barely been able to get any sleep myself. I'm starting to feel sort of like I'm in a dream-like daze. Not to mention I've missed work the last two nights. As the newest nurse, I hate to use up any time off; but I can't leave Phillip, and I sure as hell can't take him to work with me.

The man beside me lying so still on his back is too strong, too handsome and healthy to die here in my bed. I feel his cheek, and it's cooler than it has been. But I don't stop there. I trail my fingertips over his chest, down the thick arm closest to me, with biceps bigger and harder than any I've ever seen, before gliding up his stomach that's etched with muscles. Like before, the hairs on his arms stand up like he felt that even in his deep sleep, so I keep doing it. The soothing touch is starting to put me to sleep, so I lay my head down on the pillow and close my eyes.

"Don't...stop," his ragged voice says softly, making me pop up into a sitting position to look at his face. His brown eyes are cracked open, looking at me.

"You're awake!" I say in relief. When he licks his lips, I ask, "Do you want some water?"

"You. I want...you..." he grits out before his eyes close again.

"Phillip?" I say as I cup the side of his face, and he leans into my palm, rubbing against it like a cat. So, I keep touching him – his face, his chest, his arms, and occasionally even his stomach, although that makes me feel a little indecent being so close to other parts of him.

"Mmm. Feels...good. So good," he says, letting me know he's still awake. More of those goosebumps break out over his arms; but based on his words, I guess it's the nice kind.

I've never touched a man like this, just for the sake of touching him. It feels intimate in a way I've never been with anyone else. On the next tour of his body, I press my palm over the left side of his chest to feel his heartbeat. It's strong. So strong that I lay my head on his chest to listen to the thumping. And while my lips are so close to his skin, I press them to his sternum once, twice. On the third time, a big hand grabs the back of my head, startling me so that I sit up and look down at his face. His eyes are open all the way and following me, no filmy haze over the deep brown irises from pain or medicine.

"You're...alert," I say in surprise.

"You're a beautiful angel," he says all in one breath.

"I'm a nurse," I clarify with a smile. "Do you remember what happened?"

"You were touching me and kissing me."

"I...I meant the shooting," I say as heat suddenly warms my cheeks.

"Yeah, I remember. Two bullets."

"That's right. You had a fever, probably an infection, but I've been giving you antibiotics."

"Thank you," he says with a squeeze to the back of my head, reminding me his fingers are still there. "No one's ever taken care of me like this."

"No one?" I repeat, and he shakes his head.

"Not even your mother?"

He shakes his head again.

"I'm so sorry."

Phillip gives me a smile just as someone knocks on the door.

"I...I should probably go get that. It's probably Nash or one of your other friends coming to check on you."

"Okay," he agrees and starts to untangle his fingers from the back of my hair before he tugs on it again. "Wait. What's your name, angel?"

"Joanna," I tell him with a smile. "And I'm so glad you're feeling better, Phillip."

CHAPTER FOUR

Fiasco

"Oh, ah, good morning," Joanna, my guardian angel, says when I blink my eyes open and inhale the sweet scent of lavender. At least my eyes are not as heavy as the few times before when I've caught only quick glimpses of her before she disappears. Her face is close enough to kiss. And now that I think about it, my lips feel damp.

"Angel. Were you…did you just kiss me?" I ask her, my throat scratchy from sleeping for what felt like days.

"What? No, of course not," she says as she starts to move away.

"Don't. Stay," I say, reaching for her arm to see if she's real or I'm imagining her like I imagined her lips on mine and her hands on my chest and stomach. When my fingers wrap around her warm, delicate arm, I'm relieved. "You're real."

"Ah, yeah. I'm real. You've been talking to me," she replies with a grin. "How are you feeling?"

"Like last week's trash after it's been smushed in the compactor thing," I tell her honestly since I ache all over, but mostly in my side and leg. I'm afraid to even turn my head in case the pain starts up again. "Wait, what day is it?" I ask in a rush.

"It's Tuesday, why?" my angel asks.

"Shit!" I exclaim, trying to push myself into a sitting position no matter how bad it may hurt.

"What's wrong? What do you need?" Joanna asks.

"I need to go! I'm missing work, and I missed Sunday! Fuck, I never miss Sunday!"

"You're recovering from two gunshot wounds. I think your boss will give you as much time off as you need!" she says as I throw my legs over the side of the bed, gathering up the courage to try and stand on them.

"You don't understand. I don't get days off. I only get paid for the days I work, for the hours I work!" I shout as I push myself up and a jolt of fire shoots up my leg and side. "Fuck!"

"Slow down, Phillip," Joanna says, calling me by my real name. It's so unusual that it doesn't even sound right to my ears. "You can't go to work. I think Nash and the guys called in for you. They've got it all covered."

She's right about that one thing. I'm in too much pain to lift my arms to put a shirt on, so I sure as shit won't be climbing up on any roofs anytime soon. Reluctantly, I sit back down on the edge of the bed.

"Fine. I may not be able to go to work, but I do need to see someone. Can you give me a ride?" I look over my shoulder to ask her.

"I'm not sure if you're up for going out just yet."

"Please," I beg. "It's important or I wouldn't ask. Trust me, I wish I didn't have to get out of this bed, but I have to."

"Will it take long?" she asks.

"No. Just two stops, five or ten minutes at most."

Her palm comes up and cups my cheek, then slides up to my forehead like she's touched me a ton of times and it's no big deal to her, but it is to me. I like her hands on me, a little too much. "Your fever is gone." She sighs, making her pretty pink lips part, and then she says,

"Okay, we can try to go out, but only if you promise to tell me if it's too much too soon."

"Huh?" I ask since I had forgotten what we were talking about.

"You wanted to leave. Unless you changed your mind?"

"No. I do. I didn't," I say in a rush when I remember. Jesus, she's going to think I'm an idiot. And I am; I just don't want her to know that yet.

"You're still on a lot of meds," Joanna says. "They'll make your head a little foggy until they wear off."

"Oh, okay."

"So, you still want to leave even though I would rather you not?" she asks.

"Yes. Please."

"Okay, fine. I think one of the guys brought you some clothes yesterday," Joanna says, going over to a pile of things on a chair in the corner of the room and coming away with a pair of gray sweatpants and a ratty old tee shirt with so many holes it looks like Swiss cheese. "Are these yours?" she asks.

"Yeah, they're mine," I mutter, hating to claim them, but I don't think I can leave in just my boxer briefs.

Joanna, the saint that she is, helps pull the shirt gently over my head and even helps get my arms through the sleeve holes. Then she kneels down at my feet and helps get the sweatpants up to the top of my thighs. That's when her position and the fact that my dick is semi-hard and so close to her face makes things awkward.

"Your boots are still here," Joanna says before she gets up and retrieves them.

Imagining how ridiculous I'll look in my steel-toe boots and jogging pants distracts me while Joanna puts them on me with no socks, and then we're ready to go.

"Do you need help getting down the steps?" she asks when we get to her porch.

"No, I've got it," I say, gritting my teeth to force my leg to bend and move down them instead of asking for her to help support me.

When I finally sit down in the passenger side of her car, I feel like I've just run a marathon.

"So, where am I taking you that's so important?" I give her the address but nothing else. The less she knows about my fucked-up life, the better.

"Is this it?" Joanna asks when we pull up a few minutes later in front of a small, one-bedroom house with the paint chipping.

"This is it. I'll be right back," I tell her.

"Do you need me to…"

"Nope," I interrupt her offer to help me get up the three steps that look like they were made for giants. How come I never noticed that before now?

I make it up them, barely. Then ring the doorbell.

The woman who answers the door with her strawberry blonde hair pulled back in a long ponytail is still as tall and thin as always wearing nothing but a pair of tight workout shorts and a sports bra. She probably just went for a run or came back from one and will get a shower before she goes to pick up Sierra from preschool.

"Hey, Giselle," I say. "Can I come in so we can talk?"

"What the hell happened to you?" she asks, probably not because she's worried about me but because I missed Sunday, the worst possible thing I could've done.

"I got shot Friday night."

"Shot?"

"Yep."

"Okay, come in and explain," she says with a heavy sigh, which is a huge relief.

CHAPTER FIVE

Joanna

What Phillip said would take five or ten minutes turns into almost thirty. I consider going to knock on the door to make sure he's okay several times but figure the woman would come out and say something if he passed out.

When Phillip finally does come out of the house, he turns and hugs the tall, beautiful modelesque woman before he starts down the steps. I should get out and go help him, but then the woman comes out and grabs his arm to guide him slowly down the three steps.

At the bottom, he gives her a quick kiss on the lips, the two of them nearly the same height, and then she jogs back up the steps, and he slowly, gently, comes over and lowers himself into the passenger seat of my car.

He smells strongly of women's perfume or body lotion, making me wonder what he was doing in there for nearly half an hour. He wasn't...they weren't...were they? Hunt was injured but that didn't slow his dick down.

"You're too sick to have sex," I blurt out, which comes out sounding more jealous than I expected.

"Oh, well, that's too bad," Phillip says, but doesn't make any other comments about it.

He just gives me the direction to the next address, an apartment complex that's not but a mile or two away from the last house. "Are you visiting another woman here too?" I can't help but ask after I put the car in park.

"Yeah."

"Should we have stopped and bought her flowers?" I remark sarcastically.

"Flowers? Why would I get her flowers?"

"Because that's what you do when you like a woman."

"Trust me, no amount of flowers will make this woman or the last like me," he says seriously. "I'm just trying to convince them not to hate me for missing Sunday."

Frowning in confusion, I ask, "Were you supposed to see them on Sunday?"

"Yeah."

"Both of them?"

"Uh-huh."

"Do they know about each other?" I question him.

"Well, yeah, of course. The three of us get together every Sunday at two. I've never missed a single one before this past one."

Jesus. He has not one but two girlfriends?

"So, you're...never mind," I say with a shake of my head since it's none of my business.

Phillip climbs out of the car, making a few grunting sounds like it hurts and then shuts the door behind him.

I shouldn't care that he's seeing two women, or that he sees them at the same time. He's an outlaw biker who got shot. Did I expect him to actually be capable of having a normal relationship with a woman or even want someone like me?

What the hell was I thinking?

Phillip is my patient and nothing else. I need to start remembering that.

CHAPTER SIX

Fiasco

"**W**ake the fuck up! It's homecoming day, motherfucker!" Devlin exclaims as he and the other four members of the Dirty Aces MC barge into the bedroom at Joanna's house one morning.

I'm not sure why I'm surprised. Last night Joanna finally made the call, telling Nash that I've been fever free for four days, had finished up the antibiotics I needed, and that my wounds were healing great.

Still, I'm not ready to leave.

"Go to hell," I mutter covering my head with a pillow. There's an extra one since Joanna hasn't slept in her bed with me since...well, since the day I went to see Giselle and Katrina. For some reason, she's acted like she's been mad at me ever since, but she's still been taking care of me like no one else has ever done before.

"Fine we will, but we're taking you with us," Malcolm declares as he rips the pillow away from my fingers and Silas pulls the bedsheets off my body. Thankfully, I'm wearing a pair of boxer briefs or they all would've gotten an eyeful.

"Go easy on him!" Joanna warns from the doorway, just the sound of her voice making my dick twitch before I see her beautiful face. "He's still healing from two gunshots."

"I'll take his shit to the car," Nash says as he throws my clothes into a big bag. On the way out of the bedroom, I see him pull a thick envelope from his back pocket and hand it to his sister. I didn't know that until Wirth told me. Joanna still doesn't know they're related, and I'm not sure if Nash is ever planning on telling her. It's just another reason why I shouldn't have missed having her sleep next to me the past few nights.

"You've already paid me plenty," Joanna says to him.

"Take it," Nash insists. "For the time you missed from work and meds you had to steal. Least we can do."

Dammit. That makes me feel guilty since it's my fault she missed work. No wonder she's so ready to be rid of me.

"Thank you," Joanna says softly as she takes the envelope.

"No, thank you," Nash replies before he walks out of the room with my bag of clothes.

"If you all have any other medical emergencies, you know where to find me," Joanna says, meeting my eyes for a quick second before they're sadly gone.

"You're a goddamn saint," Malcolm says, kissing her cheek on the way out with Silas and Devlin behind him.

"What the fuck am I supposed to wear home?" I ask when I finally look around and remember Nash left with my clothes.

"Hold on," Joanna says before she goes to the closet. I watch her ass like a hawk, except I don't think hawks look at women and think about getting them naked and underneath them. She pulls out a blue robe and brings it over as I stand up beside the bed. I let her help pull it on just so I can be close to her this one last time.

"Nice look, man," Wirth teases. "Now let's go."

"At least you're all covered up now," Joanna looks up at my face and says when she tries to pull the two sides of the robe together, but my shoulders are too broad.

Fuck, I'm going to miss her like crazy, waking up and seeing her beautiful face every morning. That's why I do something stupid.

My hands shoot out, cradling her face gently in them to hold her still so I can bring my lips down to hers. I expect her to push me away when she realizes what I'm doing. But she doesn't. Her lips kiss me back as her hands grab on to my shoulders, and then she opens them for me to slide my tongue inside, tasting more of her, not rushing the kiss but indulging, savoring every second. When she moans, telling me she's enjoying it as much as I am, I groan into her mouth.

"Fiasco!" Wirth yells my name, making Joanna and I both jump since I didn't even consider that we may have an audience. Fuck it. I don't care.

Joanna breaks the kiss first, taking a step backward, but I can't seem to make my feet leave.

"Come on, buddy," Wirth says when he comes over and grabs my elbow to urge me to go with him. "You're still surviving two gunshot wounds. No reason to make Nash add a third or a fourth."

"It would be worth it," I say with a heavy sigh.

"What?" Joanna asks. "Why would Nash care…"

"Ah, see ya, Joanna. Thanks again for everything!" Wirth calls back to her before hurrying me out of the house.

CHAPTER SEVEN

Joanna

"**Y**ou're back!" Casey says when she finds me sitting in the hospital cafeteria pushing my fork around my salad the first day back after Phillip left my care.

"I'm back," I agree and try to give her a smile.

I haven't lived in town long, but Casey and I became good friends fast, not just because we work in the same hospital but because we're both young divorcees who bonded over our pain-in-the-ass exes. Now I guess we both have crushes on bikers.

She pulls out the chair on the other side of the table to sit down right across from me. "Does that mean that your…patient is better?"

"He's recovering well. The guys came and took him home yesterday."

"Then why does your tone of voice make it sound like he died?"

"That's ridiculous. I don't sound like that."

"You didn't want him to leave, did you?" she says with a smirk.

"Of course I wanted him to leave!" I exclaim. Lowering my voice, I tell her, "My job was to make sure he survived, and he did."

"Yeah, but now you're missing having a hot blond man in your bed."

"Casey, you know he only slept in it. Nothing happened." I remind her.

"He was unconscious the entire time I was there, but even a man like him on his death bed would try and get you out of your panties."

My face flushes in a rush, which doesn't go unnoticed by Casey. "What aren't you telling me, Joanna?"

"Nothing," I say, but that's a lie and she'll know it. "At least not much. He kissed me yesterday before he left."

"He kissed you? That's it?"

"Yes."

"And said he wanted to see you again?"

"No."

"What?" she scoffs. "Then it was just a quick peck on the cheek to say thanks and goodbye?"

"No, it was not on the cheek, and it wasn't quick," I admit, finally laying my fork down, giving up on eating lunch. "It was the kind of kiss that usually leads to much more."

"So why didn't it? Was he too sick to get it up?" She props her chin in her palm. "You know, Hunt had the same problem at first, but it was nothing a little enthusiastic oral couldn't fix..."

"Casey!" I chastise her as I glance around to make sure no one overheard. I would prefer that our coworkers not find out that she came to my house to help with our biker patients the night of the shooting, and then helped Hunt with more than his injury in my bathroom.

"What? I could've said blowjob instead of oral." She laughs at the shocked look on my face. "You take sex way too seriously, Joanna. Trust me, it was fun, and I have no regrets at all. Hunt even invited me to come visit him in Wilmington..."

"He did?" I say in surprise.

Casey rolls her eyes at me. "I know that doesn't mean much given the source. He's an outlaw biker who nearly had his head blown off in a shootout with some rivals. Still, at least he offered to see me again."

"Yes, at least he offered," I agree. "One of the other guys interrupted me and Fiasco saying something odd about how Nash would be pissed at him. Then, Fiasco just walked out without saying another word to me!"

"If you want to see Fiasco, you know where to find him," Casey points out. "Everyone knows about the Dirty Aces pool hall."

"I can't just show up there."

"Why not?"

I shake my head. "I'm not going to pursue him. That's too… desperate." Casey shrugs and looks around the cafeteria, avoiding my eyes. "What?" I ask her.

"I didn't say anything."

"But you were thinking it. Just tell me."

"Fine! I was considering going to see Hunt, even if it makes me look *desperate*."

"Really?"

"There are some benefits to having no-strings attached, crazy hot sex with an attractive man."

"And what would that be?"

"The crazy hot sex part," she says with a grin. "Women have needs too. My ex-husband spent the last few years telling me that I wasn't pretty or sexy and that no other men would want me. It's nice to finally have a little male attention, someone who thinks I'm everything he said I wasn't."

"Then maybe you should go…"

"Will you come with me?" she asks.

"No," I say without even needing to think about it. "Sorry, but I don't think I could do that. Hunt invited you, not me."

"You know Fiasco probably won't be in Wilmington. I'm sure you could find another pretty biker boy to tend to in your bed."

"I wish I was confident enough for a one-night stand, but I'm not that kind of girl and you know it."

"If you say so," Casey replies. "That will leave more bikers for me."

"More bikers? I would think that you would have your hands full with Hunt," I tell her with a grin.

Flashing a smile that would rival the Cheshire cat, she says, "Oh, Joanna. You have no idea what a handful or mouthful Hunt is!"

I hold my hands up in front of me in protest while laughing. "Nor do I ever need to know either."

She laughs and then gets up. "I'm going to find something to eat. Will you at least consider coming with me on Friday?"

For half a second, I consider getting dressed up and going with Casey to a biker bar full of rowdy men, but I just don't see that happening. I'm too shy and self-conscious. Besides, there's only one biker I want to see, and Casey's right, Fiasco probably won't be there.

CHAPTER EIGHT

Fiasco

"**Y**ou're looking pale, man. Maybe it's time to take a break," Devlin says when his shadow moves over me on the part of the roof where I'm working.

"Can't," I tell him, reaching for another nail. "Need the money."

"You also need to not pass out and break your fucking neck when you fall off the roof, Fiasco!"

"I'm fine."

"You're not fine! You just got shot less than two weeks ago!"

I stop hammering to look up at his face, not because he told me to take a break but because I honestly don't know if I can raise my arm again at the moment to hit another nail. "That's right, I haven't earned a paycheck in almost two weeks! I have to keep going whether or not my body wants me to."

"At least go get some water," Devlin suggests. "Please? I'll take over here until you get back. You know, with your luck, you'll end up in the hospital with broken bones if you fall off here, and that'll be more weeks you'll miss."

"Fine," I mutter when he kneels down and takes over the hammering.

I crawl over to the ladder on my hands and knees because I honestly don't know if my legs will hold my weight. And jeez, I'm dizzy as fuck as I climb down. I swipe my water bottle from the cooler, a big yellow monster, and sit down on the ground with my back against a tree to drink it down.

Never in my life have I felt this weak. It makes me feel like a fucking pussy. The goddamn bullet wounds are still draining me while they heal, or at least that's what Joanna told me would happen. I believe her too since she's one of the smartest people I've ever met. She also told me I shouldn't go back to work for at least four to six weeks, but that's not exactly an option.

Damn, I miss waking up in her bed that smells like lavender, seeing her beautiful face and having her take care of me all day and night. Nobody has ever done that for me before. When I was a kid, if I got sick, I had to stay home by myself while my mom and her boyfriend were at work, which meant I still had to feed myself and I was fucking lucky if we had any meds. Even the over-the-counter shit is expensive. My mom used to tell me that it would pass, whatever hurt me. Sore throat? *It'll pass in a few days.* Throwing up? *It'll be gone in twenty-four hours.* A cold? *Get your ass out of bed and get to school, Phillip. You know you can't afford to miss a day, or you won't pass this year either!*

I hated both times that I had to repeat the same grade in elementary school. Everyone in the old class made fun of me the next year when I was with the smaller kids. And the new kids picked on me for being bigger than they were because I was too stupid to move up a grade.

When I was sixteen, I finally dropped out of school. By then, my mom was never around, so she didn't know or care. Even if she did, it's not like she could've physically dragged my ass to the high school when I was a foot taller than her and outweighed her by fifty pounds.

The worst part of dropping out was no more free meals. I had to get a job at a fast-food restaurant working long, shitty hours, but at least I could sneak and eat as much food as I wanted.

"Fiasco!" Mike, our foreman, calls out, snapping me out of the daze I was in.

"Yeah, boss?" I ask when I pull myself to my feet and they actually are strong enough to hold me.

"Stop daydreaming and get back to work!" he says. "Dev is good, but he can't do the work of two men and there's rain coming tonight."

"Yes, sir," I reply, taking one last sip of water before I head back up the ladder.

AFTER THE LONGEST twelve-hour shift of my entire fucking life, I find myself driving past the street to my rundown apartment complex. I keep right on going, which I know is an idiotic move. I need to be in bed sleeping off this fatigue, not stalking a gorgeous woman.

I really don't know what the fuck I'm doing riding down Joanna's street. No matter how badly I want to see her, I doubt she wants to see me. The Dirty Aces were nothing but a burden on her, one that Nash said he regrets, but they didn't have any other option when I was dying.

I shiver at the reminder of the pain and then the days of a high fever, how it felt like I was drowning in darkness until my eyes finally opened. That's when I saw Joanna for the first time taking care of me. Kissing her before leaving yesterday was idiotic, because now I just want to do it again and I can't. She's Nash's sister, and he wants us to leave her alone.

I slow down on my bike enough to see a light on in her living room, but I don't catch even a glimpse of her as I drive by. Did I really think she would be taking out the trash or checking the mail at the exact time of night I drove by? I'm so dumb.

I turn right at the stop sign, heading for the highway, finally ready to get a shower and get to bed when a dark shadow suddenly darts in front of my bike. I hit the brakes hard to try and stop myself, but it's too late. I hit whatever it is hard enough that I go flying through the air, landing on my back with a hard thud.

It takes several long moments for the air to return to my lungs from the impact. When I can breathe again, my fingers reach out to my sides as I try to push myself up into a sitting position and I feel grass. Guess I was lucky I didn't land on the pavement or in the middle of the road. I manage to roll to my uninjured side and then push myself up to my knees, removing my helmet and tossing it down beside me to gasp in more oxygen. A few feet away from me, my bike is laying on its side in the road, the headlight shining in my direction. There's something in front of it – a large mass bigger than a cat but smaller than a person.

Shit! What the hell did I hit?

My legs are still too weak to stand on yet, so I crawl back onto the road toward the injured animal, afraid of what I'll find. Please let it be a deer or even a skunk.

When I hear a high-pitched whimper, it's an all too familiar sound. I know without a doubt what the hell I hit. My chest aches as if my ribs have been cracked wide open. I touch a puddle of liquid that smells like pennies, glad that it's dark and the light isn't shining directly on it.

Reaching forward, my fingertips touch soft fur, and the dog whines again either because it hurts or it's scared I'll hurt it again.

"I'm sorry, so sorry, girl," I say as wetness trickles down my face. I stupidly try to wipe it away which only adds the sticky substance to mix with the tears. "Fuck!" I scream not knowing what to do.

All I know is that I can't just sit here and let the poor thing die because I hit it.

Forcing myself to my feet, I bend down and try to gently lift the animal in my arms, not sure where it's safe to touch and where it's not. I hear her panting, but she doesn't whine at my touch. I'm sure if I was hurting her, she'd make some sort of outcry.

Now what the fuck am I going to do?

I've got to get us off the road, but I can't carry the dog in my arms on the bike, even if it's drivable, which I'm guessing it's probably not. Later, I'll get Wirth to come round it up, but right now the dog's life is more important than the damn bike.

I look left and right on the quiet stretch of road before my eyes are drawn back to the stop sign I just came from.

Could Joanna help? She's a nurse, and right now that's better than nothing. I start walking back in the direction of her house. And when I know I can move faster without falling, I pick up my speed until I'm jogging.

I make it up her porch, then bang my boot against the door since I can't knock with my hand without dropping the dog that feels a lot heavier than it was a few seconds ago.

The main door opens, and then she's standing there – a sight for sore eyes. Her dark hair is pulled up all cute and messy, and she's wearing a pink, spaghetti strap satin top and matching shorts. For a second, I'm so distracted by her beauty that I forget why I'm here. Then her eyes widen, and she slaps a hand over her gaping mouth in horror.

God, she must think I'm a monster for hurting an innocent animal.

"Please help her," I say through the glass door.

Joanna finally unlocks and pushes the glass door open for me to come inside.

"Phillip…what happened?"

"I hit her with my bike," I admit. "She ran right in front of me. I tried to stop. I swear I did!"

"Oh no. That's awful! Are you okay?" she asks, searching my face. "You're bleeding." Her fingers swipe my cheek and come away with a pink tint.

"I think it's all her blood, not mine," I explain. "Please, Joanna. Can you save her? You have to help her!"

"I-I don't know anything about how to care for dogs. I'm so sorry, Phillip. You need to take her to a vet."

"How…where do I go?" I ask her, my voice frantic. "My bike's down…"

"Come on," she says, grabbing her purse from behind the door. "We'll find a vet that's open all night."

"Thank you," I tell her as I turn and hurry out, down the front porch stairs and to the passenger side of her car.

Joanna opens the door for me to slip inside and then hurries around to the driver seat as if she understands and appreciates the urgency of the situation.

I cannot let this dog die. I just can't.

CHAPTER NINE

Joanna

The instant I saw Fiasco's face on the other side of my door, I was relieved that he came back. Then I saw the hurt animal in his arms and realized it wasn't a social call. He showed up on my doorstep because he needed medical help.

I drive us to the closest vet that I think is open all night. There are three cars in the parking lot and the light is still on, which I take as a good sign.

Phillip doesn't say anything. He just jumps out, shutting the passenger door with his backside and hurries to the door with the dog in his arms. As soon as I turn my car off, I join him, opening the vet's door to let him inside.

He frantically explains what happened to the woman behind the desk who shows him into an exam room.

"Lay her down gently here, and I'll go get the vet," the woman instructs him.

Phillip does what she asks, and then he moves up to stroke the dirty brown and white head, telling her, "I'm so sorry, girl. I didn't mean to hurt you."

I know that no one would want to hurt an animal, but it looks like Phillip is more distraught than even I would be, like he hit a person instead of a dog. He is absolutely frantic and obviously blames himself.

A man in a wrinkled, white dress shirt and blue tie rushes into the room. I assume he's the vet when he starts asking us questions while examining the dog. "Is he yours?"

"He?" Phillip says.

"He's a male, and since you didn't know, that likely answers my question."

"He ran out in front of me," Phillip explains. "I hit the brakes on my bike and tried to stop."

"There's no collar," the vet notices. "Probably a stray. I'll need to get some x-rays, and they're not cheap. Are you willing to take on the expense, or should we put him out of his misery?"

"Put him…" Phillip starts in a questioning tone.

"Put him to sleep, yes. That's the humane thing to do if he has internal injuries or multiple broken legs."

"No! You have to fix him!" Phillip exclaims. "He can't die because I hurt him!"

"It was an accident, Phillip," I say when I step up next to him and lay a hand on his arm, noticing the pink flesh for the first time. He's got road rash that must hurt something awful on top of still healing bullet wounds, but he's more worried about the dog.

The vet looks from me to him and then back to me again. His eyes lower from my face to my chest, which is when I realize for the first time that I'm only wearing my thin satin pajamas and nothing else. Oh, and it's very, very cold in here thanks to the air conditioning. Well, there's nothing I can do now except take a step to the right so that I'm partially hidden behind Phillip's massive body and pull my purse around to hide the left side.

Clearing his throat, the vet goes on to tell us, "I can't even give you an estimate on the cost, not until I know more about the extent of the injuries. And I'm sorry, but our office policy for situations like this is to request a thousand dollar down payment to go toward the treatment expenses. If it's more, we'll ask before treating. If there's anything remaining at the end of treatment, it will be refunded, of course."

"A thousand dollars?" Phillip asks, eyes wide in shock.

"X-rays aren't cheap for dogs or people," the vet says. "He'll also need to be given something for the pain, sooner rather than later if he's to be kept alive. And the costs could be much greater if he needs surgery…"

"I-I don't know what to do," Phillip says.

"Can you give us a moment to talk outside?" I ask the vet, who nods.

"I'll get the pain meds started. It's the least I can do until you make a decision." *And the least he can do for being unprofessional when he was ogling my boobs*, I think to myself. Although it's not his fault I left the house without putting on clothes or grabbing a jacket.

"Thank you," I tell him as I pull on Phillip's arm to try and get him to come outside with me. He doesn't budge. "Phillip? Let's get some air and talk this over."

He reaches for the dog's head and rubs it again before he finally nods and lets me pull him out of the exam room and to the parking lot.

Phillip leans against the side of my car and runs his fingers through the front of his floppy blond hair while staring at his shoes. "I don't have an extra thousand dollars."

"It's a lot of money," I agree.

"But I can't let him die!"

"I know," I agree. "It's a tough decision. But you don't want him to suffer either, do you?"

He shakes his head. "I'll find the money somewhere." Looking up, he glances over at the closed stores across the street. "Even if I have to rob one of these joints."

At first, I think I misheard him.

"You can't be serious," I say. But then I remember that he's an outlaw biker and he's incredibly desperate to help the dog. It's sort of sweet in a way but confusing, to say the least. "Phillip? You know this wasn't your fault, right? The dog ran out in front of you. It happens all the time."

"No. I can't…I *won't* let another dog die because I fucked up."

"Another dog?" I ask in confusion.

"Can you take me to my bike?" he asks. "I need my helmet or a ski mask…"

"No, Phillip! I won't let you rob a store! Are you crazy?"

"What else can I do, Joanna?" he asks. "Today was the first time I've worked in two weeks! I don't have an extra thousand dollars just lying around."

"I do," I tell him.

"What?" he looks at me with his brow furrowed. "No," he says with a shake of his head. "I can't ask you to do that."

"You're not asking. I'm telling you," I say as I go over and open the door to go back inside. When I get to the desk, I put my purse on the counter and take out my wallet before telling the woman on the other side, "I'll be putting down the thousand dollars for the dog we brought in."

"Joanna!" Phillip says when he catches up to me. "Don't." He takes the wallet from my hand.

"I can't promise I'll be able to pay more if the cost goes over a thousand," I look into his warm brown eyes to tell him honestly. "But shouldn't we at least try?"

"You've already done so much for me, angel," he says softly, his free hand lowering to his injured side.

"And Nash gave me more money than he should have for helping you," I tell him.

"Nash paid you to…" He frowns as if it suddenly occurred to him.

"Yes," I reply when I take my wallet from his hand. Opening it, I count out ten one-hundred-dollar bills and offer them to the receptionist. "The deposit for x-rays and all. If it goes over that, can you please have the vet talk to me before doing anything else?"

"Of course," she agrees and then she hands me a clipboard. "While

I get you a receipt, you can fill this out with your contact information and maybe give the dog a name?"

"Sure," I agree.

I go over and sit down on the long, cushioned bench that runs in front of the wall to start filling out the forms. I barely get my name written down when Phillip takes a seat next to me.

"How much did Nash pay you?" he asks quietly.

"Eight thousand," I answer without looking up from the form.

I get my address and phone number all put down. Then I look up at Phillip. "What do you want to name him?"

"I dunno," he answers, leaning his back against the wall and straightening his cut. "How about Ace?"

"Ace is a good name," I agree, knowing he got it from the Dirty Aces MC.

I write it all down and then get up to take the clipboard back to the receptionist.

"Thank you, and here's your receipt," she says, giving me the printout that I fold up and put into my purse. "Dr. Dallas will take care of..." she looks at the clipboard, "Ace tonight and give you a call before his shift ends at seven a.m."

"I want to stay," Phillip says.

The receptionist starts to say something, but I grab his hand to make him look at me. "You look exhausted. Did you work today?"

"Yes."

"You shouldn't have gone back to work so soon."

"I know," he agrees.

"There's nothing we can do here but wait. You may as well get some sleep while we do that so you can work tomorrow, right?"

He nods. "I guess so."

"Come on," I tell him, tugging on his hand. "Thank you for your help," I say to the receptionist when I hold the door open for him.

Thankfully, my car isn't far away because Phillip quickly turns into a drunk zombie, like he's on the brink of passing out. He even has to lean heavily against the side while he waits for me to unlock the doors, like the weight of the world is suddenly pressing down on him. It was probably the adrenaline earlier keeping him going, and now it's fizzling out.

"Ace has to make it," he says before he rests his forearms on top of the roof of my car and lays the side of his face down on them.

"I'm sure the vet will do everything he can to save him," I say as I place my palm on the back of his leather cut to rub supportively.

"I haven't had a dog or any pets in almost twenty years."

"Oh yeah?" I say with a smile he can't see because he's still using his arms as pillows. "Why not?"

"Because my mom's boyfriend killed my last dog."

"Goodness, I'm so sorry, Phillip," I tell him as my hand stills on his back. "Was it…was it an accident?"

"No. It was my fault."

I wait for him to say more, but he doesn't. He just opens the passenger door and slumps down inside, shutting it behind him.

No wonder he was so torn up about hitting a dog. He still feels guilty about whatever happened to his last pet because he thinks it was his fault it died. I think the man must have a heart as big as he is.

And while I can't exactly afford to spend a thousand dollars on a strange dog, I know that it was money well spent. I just hope the vet can save him, for Phillip's sake.

CHAPTER TEN

Fiasco

I don't know why the fuck I told Joanna about Rosie. She probably thinks I'm a monster now. If she didn't already.

I can't believe I didn't know that Nash paid her to take care of me. All this time, I thought…hell, I don't know what I thought. But then I remember the envelope he gave her the day I left her house. Of course the MC paid her. She wasn't missing work and trying to keep me alive out of the goodness of her heart.

"So, I guess I should take you to your house?" Joanna asks once she's sitting in the driver seat of her car.

I wince, because on top of the shitty night it's already been, now I have to be even more humiliated when Joanna sees where I live.

"Phillip?" she asks. I still haven't gotten used to hearing her use my real name. It's been so long since anyone has called me anything other than Fiasco, idiot, or stupid bastard.

"Yeah, my apartment," I agree and then give her the directions.

I start to have her drop me off before she pulls into the complex, but my embarrassment of her seeing the rundown shithole is nothing compared to how fucking tired I am, too tired to walk even a few extra steps.

"Thanks for putting up the money for Ace," I tell her when she pulls up in front of the door instead of a parking spot as if she knows how weak I feel. "I'll pay you back."

"That's unnecessary, especially if it involves robbing a store," she says with a smile.

"I'll pay you back with legal cash then," I promise her and then look out the car window to the crumbling building. "It may just take a while."

"Will you need a ride to work tomorrow?" she asks.

I shake my head. "No, I'll have Wirth pick up my bike; and until it's fixed, I can drive my Thing."

"Oh. Okay."

For a second, I wonder if Joanna asked about giving me a ride because she wanted to see me again, but that's just stupid. She only took care of me because Nash paid her to and she's a nice person. She's too good for someone like me. Too smart. Too beautiful. I can't help but look at her face in the glow of what few streetlights still work in the parking lot. God, I wish I could ask her to come up to my apartment with me. Even knowing she would most likely say no, I would take the chance if my apartment wasn't a disgusting wasteland.

"Sorry I had to bother you tonight," I tell her.

"I'm not," Joanna says.

I don't know if she means that or is just being kind.

"What were you doing in my part of town when you live over here?" she asks.

Shit. Of course she's smart enough to notice that. "I was...I was coming from work. We're putting a roof on a place out near you."

"Oh."

Hopefully she believes that lie. It's not like I could tell her the real reason, that I was hoping to catch a glimpse of her through her windows. That's too damn creepy to admit.

"I noticed you have some scrapes on your arms. Do you want me to park to help you clean and bandage them?"

Crap. It does sound like she wants me to invite her up to my apartment. But I doubt it's for anything half as dirty as the things I want to do with her. Besides, she's just doing what she does for a living – trying to help. I can't even imagine someone as incredible as her even sitting on my pathetic mattress on the floor, the only furniture I have, much less letting me touch her on it.

"No, that's okay," I reply. "Thanks for everything, angel." I lean over and kiss her cheek before making myself climb out of her car and up the steps to my apartment without looking back, afraid that if I see her gorgeous face again, I may drop to my knees and beg her to come upstairs with me.

~

Joanna

WELL, that settles that – Phillip doesn't want me.

I gave him several chances to invite me to stay the night with him, and he turned me down. Now I feel so ridiculous for even pushing the issue.

The disappointment soon fades to what feels like anger.

So, when I get home, I call Casey and tell her everything that happened tonight with Phillip and that it's all her fault that I made a fool of myself.

"It doesn't make sense," she says over the phone. "Why wouldn't he ask you to come up after such an ordeal? He obviously was upset and could use some…comfort."

"Because he's not interested in me that way."

"Then why did he kiss you before he left your house the other day?" she asks.

"I have no idea! But the kiss on the cheek tonight makes it absolutely clear that he doesn't want me. God, men are so…infuriating."

"They really are! So come with me to Wilmington on Friday!" Casey begs. "I don't really want to go alone, and a night out is exactly what you need. There will be plenty of men there who will sleep with you."

"How can you be so sure?" I ask.

"Because you're beautiful, sweet, and innocent. The bikers will all want to eat you up!"

"I'll think about it, okay?"

"That's more than I could get out of you earlier, so I'll take it," she says. "Forget Fiasco. Or tell him about our plans Friday and see what he does. If he wants you, then he won't approve of you going to the Knights' bar."

"Maybe," I tell her. "But I think he's made his opinion pretty damn clear already."

CHAPTER ELEVEN

Fiasco

"I didn't think it was possible, but you look even worse today than you did yesterday," Devlin says when I get to the job site the next morning. "What happened?"

"Long night," I tell him.

"You don't say that like it was a good thing," he replies with a chuckle. "I thought the only thing that ever kept you up late at night was pussy."

"No, last night it was a dog. And Joanna."

"Joanna?" Devlin exclaims. Rubbing his forehead like he has a headache, he says, "No, Fiasco. Tell me you weren't messing around with Nash's sister!"

"I didn't. I shouldn't have tried to see her," I tell him. "Fuck, I'm so goddamn stupid! I'll never be good enough or smart enough. I'll always be broke. I dropped out of high school, so I'll be doing this backbreaking bullshit work for the rest of my life! I've got two kids to support that I hardly ever see because their mamas think I'm too irresponsible. I live in a shitty apartment to make sure the kids are taken care of. There's nothing for me to offer her, so why did I think for even a second that I could ever be good enough for a woman like Joanna?"

"Jesus," Devlin mutters, blinking at me in surprise after my outburst. "I don't know what to say to all of that. I'm sorry, man. I didn't know things were that bad for you."

"Yeah, well, they are. Always have been, always will be."

Grabbing my shoulder, he says, "Shit will get better, Fiasco. Right now, you're healing some serious injuries that could've killed you. I bet things will look up soon once you're feeling better."

"Maybe, maybe not," I say with a shrug.

"Don't be too hard on yourself. At least you're one of the dads trying to take care of their kids. A lot won't even do that. That boy and girl are lucky to have you as their father."

"Hopefully they got their mamas' brains and not mine."

"I don't know your baby mamas, so I couldn't say," Devlin replies. "But I will tell you that if Nash finds out you're still seeing Joanna, he's going to be very pissed."

"Because he knows I'm not good enough for her."

"No, because he never wanted the MC to crash into her life the way it did," he explains. "She's not like us. She's a good woman, with a college degree and a nursing career she had to work really hard for. Nash wouldn't want anything to interfere with all she's got going after she was put up for adoption by the same mom and dad that gave him up."

"She doesn't even know he's her brother," I point out.

"No, and he wants to keep it that way, for her sake. The MC has rivals and enemies. It's one thing to bring a woman into the club we want to marry, one who knows what they're in for, and we can try to protect them. It's another to drag an innocent family member in, taking a chance that she could get hurt. For Joanna's sake, think with your head and not your dick for once since you're not exactly the type to settle down."

"You don't have anything to worry about. Joanna doesn't want me like that, no matter how much I wish she did. I won't touch her."

"Good," Dev says. "Because if you do and I find out, I'll have no choice but to tell Nash."

"I know," I agree.

"You really will stay away from her?"

"I didn't mean to see her last night, I swear," I tell him.

"So, you'll stay the hell away from now on?" Devlin repeats like he thinks I'm too dumb to have heard him the first time.

"I'll stay away from her," I agree. And then I remember that I still owe her for paying Ace's vet bills. It's a little after seven now, which means the vet's office should be open again.

I tried calling them several times late last night to check on him, but all I got was the answering service.

"I need to make a quick call before we get to work," I tell Dev.

He arches an eyebrow. "You better not be calling Joanna."

"I'm not. I don't even have her phone number," I tell him, which is the truth, and it sucks.

"Fine. Hurry up, though."

I walk over to my Thing for a little privacy while I make the call. Thankfully, a woman answers. When I ask for an update on Ace, she tells me he's sleeping now but should be able to go home later. One of his back legs is broken, but the vet thinks he'll be able to get around fine with it in a cast until it heals in a few weeks.

I'm so fucking relieved I didn't kill it that I could cry, but I don't since I'm at a job site.

CHAPTER TWELVE

Joanna

On the way to work, I get a call from the vet's office, the same vet last night I think, telling me that Ace is going to pull through just fine. He'll have a tiny cast on his back leg, but he is otherwise doing great.

"You can come pick him up this afternoon. I'll be back around six-thirty if you want to come then, so I can go over his care."

Since I don't have Phillip's phone number and the vet's office didn't take it down last night, I guess it is on me to pick up Ace.

"Oh, right. I'll come pick him up around six-thirty tonight when I get off work," I agree.

"I look forward to seeing you then," he says cheerfully.

Once we end the call, I try to figure out what I'm going to do with the dog once I have him. Do I take him to Phillip's? He seemed pretty adamant about adopting him, and it will be a good excuse to see him again tonight, even though he would probably rather see the dog than me.

~

"HERE HE IS, almost as good as new," Dr. Dallas, the vet, jokes when he carries Ace into the exam room and puts him on the table that evening. Ace tries to sit on his back leg and then whimpers when the cast on the right hind leg gets in the way. He flops down on his other side..

"Aww, poor guy," I say as I rub his head and then around the white of his chin and neck.

"I'll send some pain meds home with him. He can have one in the morning and one at night if he seems uncomfortable."

Ace's tongue swipes out and licks at my finger while his big, brown eyes stare up at me so sweet and innocently, reminding me of someone else I recently took care of while they were injured. After the first taste of my hand, he comes back for more, licking and licking until I pull away.

"Okay, buddy. I don't know you well enough for a tongue bath," I laugh as I rub his ears, keeping out of reach of his now panting tongue.

"He's a stray you and your…boyfriend hit last night?"

I look up at the vet and shake my head. "Yes, he's a stray, but Phillip is just a friend."

"Oh," Dr. Dallas responds. "Well, he seems to have a good temperament."

"Who, Ace or Phillip?" I joke with a smile.

"Ace," he answers with a grin. "I'm guessing he's a boxer mixed with something a little bigger, about six or so months old, which means he'll need to be neutered soon unless you want him to father litters all over town."

"Oh, right," I agree.

"We can wait until his leg's recovered since I don't think he'll be wandering too far until he heals. When I see you back to take his cast off, we can set a date."

"Sure, that sounds great," I tell him as I keep scratching Ace's head.

He closes his eyes and looks like he's smiling with his tongue lolling out one side of his mouth.

"Then I look forward to seeing you in a few weeks, unless I can convince you to let me take you to dinner this weekend?"

"Ah, what?" I ask, looking away from the dog's face to the vet's. *Did he just ask me out?*

"Would you like to have dinner with me? I work the night shift during the week but not on weekends."

"Oh," I reply in surprise. I guess Dr. Dallas liked my satin pajamas more than I expected last night. I'm a hot mess this evening too in my wrinkled scrubs and my hair falling out of my ponytail after my long shift.

"How about I give you my number? You can think about it and call me if you're interested?" he asks when I don't respond with a yes or a no. I think I'm too surprised because there has only been one man on my mind for the past week or so.

"Sure," I agree, because it's the polite thing to say. When Dr. Dallas pulls out a business card from his dress shirt pocket, I look at him from the prospective as a date and not a veterinarian. He's most likely in his mid to upper thirties with dark brown hair kept short and neat. While he's nowhere close to Phillip's towering height, he still has a few inches on me and is lean like a runner or a professional man who works in an office all day and doesn't have to or want to lift anything heavy. I would even say he's attractive, but I just don't see the spark of potential in him as more than a friend.

Guess I've developed a sudden addiction to bad boys.

CHAPTER THIRTEEN

Joanna

When I get to Phillip's apartment building, I realize that I don't even know which one is his. I put Ace down on the patch of sandy grass over near the entrance with his new red collar and leash on him to see if he needs to go to the bathroom while I try and figure out what to do.

I can't go door to door knocking on each one to ask. The vibe I get from this neighborhood is not a good one – like more than one renter could open the door with a gun pointed at me.

I'm sure someone as big and tough as Phillip wouldn't worry about the armed neighbors, but I do.

"Who are you?" a man asks when he comes out of one of the first-floor apartments. There's a cigar hanging out of the corner of his mouth, the rest of his face wrinkled and grumpy looking with only a light fringe of white hair around his bald head.

"Hi, I'm Joanna."

"I don't remember you. Who are you living with? I'm supposed to be told when someone new moves in!" he says angrily.

"Oh, I don't live here. I'm just visiting someone," I say with a smile.

"Who would that be?" he asks.

"Phillip…" I start and then pause since I don't know his last name.

"Phillip? I ain't got no renters here named Phillip."

"What about Fiasco? Do you know him?" I reply since not even his friends in the MC knew his real name.

The old man blinks at me and then his narrowed eyes become slightly more pleasant. "Yeah, I know Fiasco. He's a member of the Dirty Aces. The boy doesn't cause me trouble and pays his rent on time. He's even helped me run off the assholes who think they can live here for free." Removing his cigar to blow out the smoke from his mouth, he comes closer and takes in every inch of me from my ponytail to my white shoes. "You don't look like the usual type of girl he has visiting."

Since I'm not sure what he means by that, I don't respond.

"Still, no pets allowed, especially loud ass barking dogs."

Well, crap. Did Phillip know that? I think he would've mentioned it since he was so adamant about taking care of Ace.

I look down at the dog on the end of the leash lying in the grass, staring up at me, and know that I'm already a goner. I'll be taking him home with me even though I'm hardly ever there.

"Can I bring the dog to visit Phillip once in a while?" I ask the man, who I'm guessing is the owner or super.

"There's no Phillip who lives here, woman," he starts and then says, "Oh, you mean Fiasco?"

"Yes, Fiasco," I agree even though I hate that everyone calls him the name meant to be an insult.

"Ah, I guess so, long as you clean up after it," he agrees.

"Thank you," I tell him with a smile.

"He should be home soon. I could let you in his place so you can wait there in case the rain comes early."

"That would be great, thanks," I say when I pick up Ace in my arms.

"I'm Ray, Ray Bullins," he tells me as he shuffles his feet toward the stairs. "I own these apartments."

"Nice to meet you, Ray." I follow behind him slowly up the steps, which is fine since Ace is no lightweight. Thankfully, he stops at the second door on the second floor and doesn't go up to the third.

Pulling out a huge keyring that's attached to his belt, he finds the right one and turns it in the lock. "There you go."

"I appreciate your help."

"No skin off my back," he replies with a shrug. "Not like the idiot has anything worth stealing even if you weren't a nice woman."

"He's not an idiot," I tell him firmly. "And his name is Phillip, not Fiasco. So, stop calling him that."

"Whatever you say, ma'am," he says with a smile as he backs away and I step into the apartment.

I'm not sure what I was expecting. From the exterior of the building, I knew these were not brand new, luxury apartments by any stretch of the imagination. But there's no furniture in the place at all. There's a mattress on the floor with sheets pulled up over it neatly and a few upside-down cardboard boxes that serve as a table for a lamp and a bigger one as a stand for an old tube television, the kind my parents had but I haven't seen in fifteen or so years since I bought them a new one for Christmas the first year I had a job.

In the kitchen is an old cream-colored refrigerator, and I don't have to open it to guess there's not much inside. There's a small stove and microwave, and that's it. That's all the contents of the open room.

Poor Phillip. No wonder he was in such a hurry to get back to work, even though he needed weeks to recover from the bullet wounds. He must barely be able to get by as it is, living paycheck to paycheck.

I know from experience what it feels like to be poor, and lately I haven't been able to pay all of my bills on time since I got a divorce and started living on my own. But my situation is nothing compared to this.

Ace's panting reminds me that he's in my arms and getting heavier. I lower him to the worn beige carpeted floor that looks like it was installed twenty or more years ago and then go to the kitchen to find something to put some water in for him. The cabinets are nearly bare, and I know because some are missing doors. But I do find a stack of colorful bowls. The water coming out of the faucet is sort of a reddish-brown color at first, so I let it run until it turns clear, or at least only a little cloudy before I fill up the bowl.

"Here you go, boy," I say to Ace as I put the bowl down on the other side of the fridge. When I straighten, a pair of photos taped to the refrigerator catch my eye. One is of a smiling girl who looks maybe three or four. Beside her is a picture of a boy maybe a year or two older. The two have nearly identical blonde curls, along with big brown eyes that are the same color and shape as Phillip's.

Are they his son and daughter? No, he would've mentioned if he had children, wouldn't he? Maybe they're his niece and nephew.

The apartment door suddenly opens, making me gasp as I spin around toward it. I'm not the only one caught off -guard. In the blink of an eye, Phillip has a gun out and pointed at me.

"Jesus, Joanna!" he exclaims as he lowers the weapon to his side and closes his eyes like he's taking a deep, calming breath. When he opens his dark brown eyes again, they look angry instead of startled. "What the hell are you doing in my apartment?"

"I'm sorry we scared you. Ray just let us in to wait," I say and then squat down next to Ace to rub his head.

"Fuck!" he says, shoving the gun into the back of his pants, which I guess is where it was before. "I thought Ray was psychic or some shit. He saw me coming in and told me no dogs allowed, and I thought he was just reading my mind. He could've mentioned he let you up here!"

"Sorry," I say again.

"How would you feel if someone barged into your place?" he asks.

"I would be upset too I think," I respond. "I should've waited downstairs, I know. I picked up Ace from the vet and thought you would want to see him. I thought you wanted him. Didn't you know about the no pet policy?"

"No," he answers as he comes over and kneels on the floor on the other side of Ace. As soon as he touches him, his tense shoulders seem to relax and some of the anger eases out of him. He frowns when he sees the cast; but when Ace rolls to his back wanting a belly rub, Phillip smiles down at him. "I'm glad you're okay, buddy," he says to him. Then to me, "I'll pay you back and help find him a home."

"Oh, well, I thought I would just keep him," I respond.

"You will?" he asks with what sounds like relief. "You don't have to do this. You've already paid a huge vet bill. I can't ask you to take him in too."

"I want to," I say as I reach over and rub his belly. "He seems sweet."

"Yeah, he does," Phillip agrees with a smile.

"But I may need your help," I tell him.

"What do you mean?"

"I work long hours at the hospital. I get a few days off at a time, but I'll need someone to let him out when I'm working, take him for walks, make sure he has food and water. I could give you a key to my place."

"You want me to go into your house when you're at work to take care of him?" he asks.

"If you have time? Or you could come when I'm there just to visit him, anytime you want."

"Why would you trust me that much? You have nice things; and as you can see, I'm broke as fuck. I barely have a penny to my name."

"If you tell me I can trust you, then I will," I explain. "Besides, I doubt a lock would keep someone like you and the MC out if you wanted in bad enough."

"That's true enough," he says with a grin. "I could definitely take care of Ace at lunch and on breaks if a job site is close to your place, but I can't make any promises. Just, don't come back here."

"Why not?" I ask in a huff. "You don't want to see me, just Ace?"

"What? No," he says in a rush and then clenches his jaw. "I mean, I'm not supposed to see you, but that doesn't mean I don't want to keep seeing you. But my place is a shithole. Why would you want to come back?"

The fact that he's admitted that he's embarrassed about his apartment means a lot. Which is why I tell him, "I was adopted when I was a baby by an older man and woman who were farmers. They were nice to me, but they could barely get by. We didn't have much and nothing new ever. I think they adopted me so that I could take care of them and help out at the farm, not because they wanted a daughter. It was sometimes lonely without a brother or sister or anyone my age to play with or talk to. Growing up like that made me appreciate everything I have now."

"I'm sorry, that sounds a lot like me growing up in a trailer park," Phillip says. "Too bad your parents didn't adopt Nash too, then you could've had your brother with you and some help on the farm."

His eyes widen as soon as the words leave his mouth like he said too much. I replay his last statement and try to figure out what he thinks he shouldn't have said.

"Nash was adopted too?" I ask him, and he nods. "But why do you think...why did you say he's my brother?"

"Fuck, Nash is going to kill me." He scrambles to his feet, and I do the same. "Please don't tell him I told you."

"Are you serious? Nash is my brother?" I haven't seen him in days, but just thinking about the man makes me remember his eyes and hair that are similar to the ones I see in the mirror every day. "Phillip, is he really my brother?" I ask since he hasn't said anything while I was lost in thought. He's just pacing back and forth in his nearly empty apartment, running his fingers through his floppy blond hair.

Finally, he stops pacing and looks at me, his shoulders slumped in defeat. "Yes. I wasn't supposed to tell you that, though! He didn't want you to know."

"Why not?" I ask. "Did he know...he knew that night that you showed up at my house? He tracked me down, knew I was not only a nurse but his biological sister?"

"Yes."

"That-that asshole!" I exclaim. Why would he do that? God, I feel so stupid for not realizing it sooner.

I need to leave, to get some air. I start for the door, and then remember the reason I was there in the first place — Ace.

Going over to where he fell asleep during our argument, I scoop him up to leave.

"Could you please get the door?"

"You're leaving?" Phillip asks from behind me.

"Please open the door. My hands are full, as you can see."

"Joanna, don't leave when you're pissed."

"You should've told me!" I yell at him.

"Nash told me not to, and he had a good reason."

"Oh yeah? What reason?" I blink back the tears in my eyes, angry and hurt that they knew this from the very first day and didn't tell me. I guess Nash never wanted a sister; he just wanted someone who could patch up his friends.

"He never meant to drag you into the MC's business. You pulled the bullets out of me. You saw how dangerous shit can be for us."

"He used me. You used me like your own little private hospital!" I yell at him, which is when he finally opens the door and lets me escape.

CHAPTER FOURTEEN

Joanna

I drive around aimlessly in the dark, rainy night for hours until Ace whines from the passenger seat. Of course, he probably needs to go to the bathroom. It's going to take some time before I get used to having someone else's needs to constantly consider. But that's not actually a bad thing. I have been lonely on my own since the divorce. It'll be nice to have someone to come home to, even if he runs on four legs.

Maybe I was unknowingly circling the area or maybe it was fate that we were on the street right outside of the Dirty Aces pool hall. I take it as a sign that I should go in after Ace handles his business.

He takes forever in the pouring rain, searching for the perfect spot to finally squat awkwardly since he can't exactly lift his back leg. Then I'm hurrying him under the awning as fast as his three legs can take him. On the dry part of the sidewalk, Ace shakes his short fur to dry it and then lays down in protest. I guess I'll be carrying a wet dog inside with me.

There are a few men sitting at the bar, but none of them wearing the leather vests of the MC. I do recognize the man playing pool with a blonde woman in a very short dress. At least, they're holding pool sticks, but I don't think the way he's bending over her, kissing her neck is part of the game.

"Wirth!" I say, and he jumps up and turns around to face me with the stick in his hand.

"Who is she?" the woman with him asks.

"Maeve, doll, this is Joanna. She's…a nurse who helped heal the guys after the shooting," he says, although it sounded like he started to say something else. "Joanna, this is my girlfriend, Maeve."

"Aren't you forgetting another word you should use to describe me to your girlfriend?" I ask.

"Ah, no, no I'm not," he says with a shake of his head before he turns to Maeve. "I swear, it's not what you think. I haven't ever touched her!"

After his plea, I realize my words sounded like a jealous woman and not what I intended.

"I meant sister, as in Nash's sister," I clarify.

"Oh shit," Wirth says softly and then calls out, "Nash! You've got a visitor."

"That's right, Nash. Your sister is here to see you!" I add when the tall, dark and handsome man comes out of one of the rooms cautiously.

"Hi, Joanna," he says quietly, and then he shoves his hands into the front of his jean pockets, trying to look sweet and innocent. "How did you find out?"

"Phillip just told me! Why didn't you?" I yell at him even though I'm guessing it's a little hard to look indignant with my arms full of a wet dog and the rain dripping down my hair to my face.

Nash's brow wrinkles in confusion and then his eyes narrow. "What the fuck were you doing with Fiasco?"

"That doesn't matter! And his name is Phillip!" I say, growing even angrier at him for being upset with the other man. I was a few hours ago, but only because he kept this from me. I can almost bet that

Phillip didn't tell me because Nash ordered him not to. While I'm not entirely sure of the MC's whole ranking system, I'm certain Nash has more authority in the MC than Phillip. "You should have told me we were related from the beginning!"

"What's all this shouting about?" another man asks when he comes out of the room Nash just left wearing the same leather vest and jeans. It doesn't take long for me to recognize his shoulder length brown hair and tattoos up and down his arms. Malcolm, the MC's president. "Joanna?" he says in surprise. "Why the fuck did you bring a dog into our bar?"

"Long story," I say with a sigh. "But since Nash here has been stalking me, maybe he can fill you in!"

"I wasn't stalking you," Nash says. "Lucy, my girlfriend, found you and the records about you being a nurse. I wasn't planning to ever bother you; but on the night of the shooting, you were our only option. Malcolm and Hunt would've survived but not Fiasco. Would you have rather we let him die?"

I wince at the thought of what would've happened to Phillip, if they hadn't gotten him to me in time. I would have never had a chance to help him or talk to him or kiss him…

"I don't care that you brought them to my place. What I care about is that you lied about how you knew who I was and that I was a nurse! You should've told me everything from the beginning."

"That night was hectic," Nash says. "I didn't want to distract you from sewing Fiasco up with the bombshell that we had the same mother and maybe the same father. I couldn't take your attention away from the patients for their sake."

"So, you might be my brother, not just half-brother but…" I'm unsure what to say to that, so I sort of rock the wet dog in my arms like a baby, more to calm myself than him since he seems content to just be held.

"Yes," he answers. "There was no father listed on your birth certificate, but there was on mine. Lucy found records showing that both of them lived at the same address all those years…"

"They were living together, like a couple, and they just decided to give up not one baby but two? Why?"

"I wish I knew," Nash replies with a heavy sigh.

"Were they young?"

"In their twenties."

"So not teenagers."

"No, not teenagers," he says with a shake of his head.

"They just didn't want us?"

He shrugs. "Maybe they thought they were doing us a favor, letting another family adopt us and give us a better life."

"The family that adopted me was nice enough, but we were poor as fuck," I admit.

"At least you got adopted. I bounced around foster homes, nothing ever permanent."

"Jesus," I mutter. "I'm sorry," I tell him and then laugh. "I came here pissed at you, and somehow I'm the one apologizing."

"I'm sorry I didn't tell you after the crisis was averted. I should have, but I didn't know if you would want to know me. Not to mention that we had already dragged you into the MC's business more than we should have. Keeping you apart from all this is for your safety."

"I'm tougher than I look, Nash. And of course, I would want to know my brother, as long as you're not a serial killer or anything," I joke.

He cringes and keeps his gaze on the floor. "In that case, you should probably leave and stay away from me."

"What?" I ask in confusion as I look at the other two men's faces and they quickly go about their business, Wirth back to teaching pool and Malcolm to the bar to grab a drink, both pretending like I'm not there. "You're joking, right? You seem like such a nice guy…"

"Looks can be deceiving," Nash says softly before he disappears back into the other room, leaving me standing there making a puddle of rainwater on the floor, trying to figure out what he meant by that statement.

What did he mean? Was he being serious about killing people? God, men are so infuriating, even ones I'm apparently related to.

There's no trying to blink back the tears this time, I let them fall as I turn to leave.

CHAPTER FIFTEEN

Fiasco

Despite how exhausted my body feels after a shower, aching from work and desperately needing sleep, I know I won't be able to get any until I make sure Joanna is okay.

Since Nash, Wirth, and Malcolm have been blowing up my phone even though I'm obviously avoiding their calls, I'm guessing she went to the bar and confronted her brother.

I hate having her mad at me. It's a common occurrence with women; but for some reason, it bothers me that someone as good and kind as Joanna is angry at me and hurting because of my big mouth.

Even though it's eleven o'clock at night and the rain is pouring outside, I hurry down to the parking lot, get in my Thing, and drive over to Joanna's place.

Her car is in the driveway; but as I knock on her door for the third time, I start to think she may not answer it. I'm about to leave when the main door opens and she's standing on the other side of the glass in a fuzzy, white robe with little purple hearts on it.

The annoyed look on her beautiful face warns me that the first words out of her mouth will probably be to tell me to leave.

"What are you doing here, Phillip?" she asks, her voice slightly muted by the glass.

I try to find a response that will most likely win her over. "You told me I could come visit Ace anytime I wanted."

She scowls at me for several silent seconds until I brush the front of my wet, dripping hair back. Then, finally, for some reason, her face softens, and she opens the glass door and holds it open for me to come inside.

Joanna goes into the living room while I'm still trying to dry my boots on the welcome mat and comes back with Ace in her arms and the leash connected to his collar. "Fine, Ace probably needs to go to the bathroom."

I glance toward the hallway and ask, "You want him to take a shit on the toilet?"

Finally, she smiles and says, "I don't know if you're joking or not, but no, Phillip, can you please take him outside?"

"Oh, yeah, sure," I reply as I lift the dog from her arms and carry him out the front and put him down in the yard. He looks up at me like, *What the hell, man. It's wet as shit out here.*

"You're not the only one getting drenched," I tell him. "Go do your business, boy!"

He waddles off, tugging on the leash as he goes to the bushes and squats down next to one. It's too dark to tell what he's doing; but when he comes hobbling back to me, I pick him up and carry him back inside.

Joanna is waiting at the door with an arm full of towels. She uses the first one on Ace. "That's as dry as he'll get," she says when she's done. "I made him a bed in front of the sofa if you want to put him down there."

I take him over to where she said and find a round doggy bed next to a bowl of water and food. She just brought him home from the vet today and she's already taking care of him.

"There you go, buddy," I tell him, rubbing his head. He circles around once before flopping down, laying his chin on his paws and closing his eyes like it's lights out for him.

"You're dripping wet," Joanna says as I stand up, and then she reaches up with another towel to dry my face and then my hair. I could take the towel from her to dry myself off, but I prefer to let her take care of it for me.

"I didn't just come over here to see Ace," I tell her.

"You didn't?" she asks, her chocolate eyes flicking to mine for a second before they lower to where she's moving the towel down to dry my arms and then the front of my leather cut.

"No, angel. I wanted to see if you were okay."

"I went to the pool hall," she says.

"Did you talk to Nash?"

"I did."

"And you're still mad at him?"

"Yep," she answers. "But I don't want to talk about me."

"Okay," I agree.

Finally, she stops patting me dry to look up at my face. She's so small and fragile-looking, like I could pick her up and carry her around everywhere like she does to Ace.

"Who were those children on your refrigerator?"

For a second, her question catches me off-guard, because I don't think there have ever been any kids on top of my refrigerator. But then I realize she's referring to the photos taped to it.

Fuck.

Well, if being a member of the MC, being dirt poor, injuring an innocent dog, and keeping the fact that she has a brother from her didn't push her away, this will for sure.

"Are they your niece and nephew?" Joanna asks when I don't say anything.

"No. They're my son and daughter, Asher and Sierra." I can't help but smile as I say their names. I'm not ashamed of them even if they'll probably grow up ashamed of me. I love them more than anything in the world, but I know having kids with two different women is probably a major deal breaker for a smart, beautiful woman like Joanna.

Most men would've learned from their mistake the first time they knocked up a woman by not wearing a condom. Two is just utter stupidity on my part. I don't have an excuse, just got too caught up in the moment to think about protection.

"You have a son and a daughter?" Joanna repeats as if she can't believe it.

"Yep. Asher just turned four and Sierra's three."

"Do they live with their mother?"

"Asher lives with his mother, and Sierra lives with hers, yeah."

Joanna's eyes widen. "Two different women?"

"Uh-huh. I only get to see them for an hour or so every Sunday."

"Every Sunday?"

"Yep."

"You mean, those two women that you saw that day that I drove you were their mothers?" she asks, and it takes me a few seconds to remember what she's talking about. I was still healing and pretty fucking high on pain killers, so I barely remember her driving me to see them both and grovel for them to forgive me for missing our weekly date.

"They were pissed that I didn't meet them at the playground or call them because I give them money every Sunday too. But once I showed them the bullet wounds and gave them the cash I was paid that Friday before it all went down, they were less pissed."

"So, you're not in a relationship with either of them?" she asks.

"God, no. They were one-night stands, and now they barely tolerate me an hour a week."

"Why only an hour a week?"

"They don't trust me to be alone with the kids. I can't blame them. Hell, I thought you wanted me to put the dog on the toilet when you asked me to take him to the bathroom, Joanna!"

She purses her lips like she's fighting a smile because she knows I'm right.

"I love Sierra and Asher, but I could never be a real father to them, so I just give their mamas as much money as I can to help them get by."

"You're a good man to do that, Phillip," Joanna says. "An hour a week and you pay child support; that's more than some fathers ever do for their children."

"It's not like court required child support though," I explain. "I give them both five hundred every Sunday."

"A thousand every week?" Joanna exclaims.

I nod. "There's good money in construction, mostly because it's back-breaking work that most people never want to do," I tell her. "So, I give them as much as I can and still make rent, even if I have to live on peanut butter and jelly sandwiches until the next Friday when I get paid again."

"Oh, Phillip," Joanna says like she thinks I'm pathetic. But then she drops the towel in her hands to grab my face, pulling my lips down to hers.

The kiss catches me off guard. After all she knows about me, I can't believe Joanna would want to touch me, much less want to kiss me.

I shouldn't have come over here.

I should've stayed away like Dev told me to do.

But the reason I didn't was because this is exactly what I wanted to happen. And before Joanna comes to her senses, I'm going to enjoy the hell out of it.

I wrap my arms around her waist to pull her closer as I part her lips with my tongue and plunge it into her mouth. God, she tastes like heaven. I could kiss her for hours, days even, and never get enough.

And while I want to rip her robe off and anything she's wearing underneath, I'm also scared shitless of what happens next. That's never happened to me before. Usually, it's nothing more than get both of us naked, put the rubber on, and shove my cock inside as hard and fast as possible. The women I've been with seem to like when I fuck their brains out and beg for more, but I don't think Joanna would. What if I'm too rough with her or she doesn't enjoy herself? This could be the only chance I get to be with her, and I don't want to screw it up.

Joanna pulls away laughing, and I think I've already fucked things up. Then she says, "You're too tall to keep kissing like this."

I smile because I don't think she's criticizing my height, just telling me it's inconvenient for long, passionate kisses.

"Do you…would you want to go to the bedroom?" she looks up and asks me hesitantly.

"I shouldn't want to," I admit, and her eyes lower. "But I want you so fucking bad," I tell her honestly.

"Good, because I want you too, Phillip," she says with a smile as she takes my hand and leads me to the bedroom.

The tidy girly room, of course, reminds me of when I was in so much pain I thought I was going to die. I never thought I would be in this room again with Joanna, at least not unless I was shot again.

"Let's get you out of these wet clothes," Joanna says as she pushes my leather cut down my arms and off before helping me get my t-shirt over my head. After I toss the shirt on the floor, I notice Joanna's eyes and hands are on my chest, her fingertips rubbing in soft circles as she stares at me. I remember her doing the same while I was in and out of sleep that week I was hurt. Her touch is so soothing, like she could've healed me with her hands alone.

I let her keep at it until her fingers lower to undo my belt and the front of my jeans. Then she pushes them down my legs as she sinks to her knees. Seeing her in that position, fuck, I know I won't last even a second in her mouth, so I pull her up.

"What…" she starts to say, but then I untie her robe and pull it apart to find a short, white satin gown underneath. The thin material can't hide how amazing her tits look; nipples so hard it looks like they hurt. I drop to my knees to cover one of them with my mouth, making Joanna cry out above me. My legs are sort of trapped in my pants around my ankles thanks to my boots, but I don't give a shit right now.

"God, Phillip," she says softly. Her fingers thread through my hair, pressing me to her body and not away as I flick my tongue over one nipple and then the other. Then it's Joanna who is getting out of her robe like it's on fire to lift the satin over her head so that she's standing naked in front of me in nothing but a pair of matching white satin panties. I give those sexy panties the same treatment as her gown, covering her mound with my mouth through the material.

"Oh my God, please!" Joanna moans, her fingers tightening on my hair. She doesn't take off the panties, so I don't either, enjoying teasing her pussy with my tongue through them until Joanna's hands let go of my hair to slap against the mattress behind her for balance as her legs give out. I lift her by her thighs to help her sit down. Then, I hook my fingers in either side of the elastic waistband to slowly pull them down her legs and off.

I run my palms up both of her smooth legs, then spread them wide so I can fit my shoulders between them. Leaning forward, I run my tongue up her slit, making her squirm and try to close her legs. I dig my fingers into her thighs tighter to hold them where I want them while licking every inch of her.

"Oh! Please! Oh God!" Joanna moans and writhes before she finally lays back on her bed.

Her hips try to bounce all over the place, but I keep holding her still, flicking my tongue over her clit until she's thrusting her body toward my mouth faster and faster. It doesn't take long for her back to arch. She screams wordlessly to the ceiling while her body jerks uncontrollably. I keep her pleasure going for as long as I can, watching her, tasting her, so fucking hard I may come from eating her pussy.

But then Joanna is urging me up off the floor. I get to my feet and quickly yank my boots off so I can remove my pants and boxer briefs. Then, when I'm finally naked, I stand between her legs. Taking myself in my hand, I rub the head of my cock through her soaking wet folds making her squirm further back on the bed, so I have to chase her.

"I need you, Phillip," Joanna says breathlessly.

I'm nearly lost to the lust as I look down at her beautiful sexy body laid out ready and waiting for me. But I do remember to grab a condom from my discarded jeans and roll it on before I crawl up the bed.

When I'm holding myself up above Joanna, her legs spread for me to fit between them, I hesitate before I kiss her since some women don't like that after oral. I should've known that Joanna wouldn't care when she grabs the back of my head to pull my mouth down to hers. I go eagerly, kissing her with a frantic tongue while my cock pushes against her entrance. I need to know how tight she is first before I slam inside, so I slip my hand between our bodies to ease my middle finger inside of her.

Joanna gasps into my mouth as I thrust the digit in and out of her a few times before adding a second finger.

"Mmm," she says before breaking our kiss. Reaching down herself, she fists my cock and says, "You. I want all of you."

I remove my fingers so she can guide me inside her heaven. Fuck, she's so hot and tight, clenching around my cock and lifting her hips to work me in deeper.

"Slow, angel, slow," I beg her. "You feel too fucking good."

"Okay, slow," she agrees and lets me set the pace.

Usually, I'm all for fast and furious, but not this time. With Joanna, I don't want to hurry up and reach the finish line. I want to make it good for her, have her come on my cock first.

CHAPTER SIXTEEN

Joanna

Nothing has ever felt as good as having a big muscular man like Phillip on top of me, pinning my hips to the bed as he moves inside of me. Each stroke hits so deep that I cry out in pleasure as my body tightens all over, so close to another orgasm while I'm still so incredibly sensitive from the last. I can't remember the last time a man went down on me, and wow, I'm not sure if it ever felt as good as when Phillip's tongue was inside of me. This second orgasm keeps growing and building until it's nearly painful before the hot warmth inside of me finally bursts open.

"Yes! Oh, Phillip! *YES!*" I scream as I tremble under his body and around his long, thick cock.

"God, Joanna," he whispers against my ear before he shoves deep one last time. His large frame stills on top of me before I feel his entire body shudder and groan with his release.

All of his weight presses down on me like a heavy blanket before he climbs off and lays down beside me on his back. I roll to my side to face him like he's the sun and I want to be as close to him as possible.

"That was…" I try to find the words to describe being with him but there aren't any. "It's been so long since I…but it was never like that," I tell him as I run my fingertips up and down his smooth, muscular chest that's still rising and falling rapidly as I cuddle up to his uninjured side.

"It was…different," he says.

"Different?" I repeat since I can't tell by the tone of his voice if he means that in a good way or a bad way, making me feel suddenly self-conscious.

"Better," he amends. He throws his arm around me and his fingers play with my hair. "The best ever."

That makes me smile. "Best ever? I bet you say that to all the girls."

"Not that I can remember," he replies. "And right now, I'm having a hard time remembering any woman I was with before you."

I smile even wider but don't press him further since my ego is satisfied with his words.

We lay there together, listening to the rain pounding on the windows and roof outside. I wouldn't want to be anywhere but here with him. For a moment, I wonder if he's trying to figure out a way to leave, so I decide to just ask him instead of wonder.

"Do you want to stay the night since it's raining and messy out?"

"I would stay even if it was beautiful and sunny out," he says.

"Good."

"Nash probably won't like me being here with you, but I don't really give a shit."

"Me either," I agree. He holds me to him a little tighter and then kisses the top of my head.

I wait for him to say more; and when he doesn't, I decide to ask what I'm dying to know. "Hey, Phillip?"

"Yeah, angel?" he asks while brushing my hair over my shoulder and running his fingers through it.

"How violent is the MC?"

"Why?"

"Just wondering what sort of things you all do. I mean, I knew you were not saints when people shot at you and almost killed you."

"The shooting was a misunderstanding with the Irish. It's all worked out now."

"Oh yeah?"

"Yeah."

"But it's not the first time the MC got violent, right?"

"God, no."

"I assumed as much," I say, and then I can't help but ask the question still on my mind from earlier tonight. "Did Nash kill someone?"

Phillip's hand freezes in mid stroke, then falls to cup my shoulder. "Why would you ask me that?"

"Because you're his friend and you're in the MC together."

"Please don't make me answer that question."

"Why not?" I push myself up to look down at his face.

"Because if I answer honestly, then you might ask me the same question. I don't want to lie to you. I don't think I could even if I wanted to."

"I don't want you to lie to me either. Could you please just tell me the truth? Earlier tonight, when I was confronting Nash, I mentioned that I would always want to know my brother, unless he was a serial killer. It was a joke, but then he told me I should leave and stay away."

"Oh. Are you going to stay away from him?" he asks, his brown eyes sad because he thinks that if he answers truthfully about Nash that I may not want to be around him either.

"Should I?" I ask. "None of the guys in the MC that I've met made me nervous or scared, like I should worry about them hurting me."

"None of us would hurt you."

"Then answer the question, for you and Nash," I tell him.

He stares at my face for several long seconds, and I expect him to say no. But then his large hand cups the back of my head and pushes it back down so my cheek is against his chest. "I'll tell you, but I don't want to see the disgust on your face when you find out the truth." His other hand wraps around my back, pressing me to him. "I'm not sure I could let you go even if you try to leave either."

"Okay," I agree since I'm not sure if I would be able to leave his arms no matter what he says, which is a scary thought since we haven't known each other that long and tonight's the first night we've slept together. I shouldn't feel so close to him so soon, but I'm not sure my heart had a choice in the matter.

"Devlin is another member of the MC. I think you met him," Phillip says. "He had just started dating this girl, Jetta, and then we found out that her brother had some gambling debt with the MC."

"Oh my god! You killed her brother?" I ask and try to lift my head. His strong hand won't let me.

"No, no. That asshole is still alive, I swear," Phillip says. "Just listen to the whole story without jumping to any conclusions, okay?"

"I'll try," I agree.

"Jetta paid off her brother Sean's debt, but the idiot got in deeper with a bad guy, a man known for drug trafficking and sex trafficking. So, Sean made a deal with the bad guy – his debt would be paid off if he could have a night with Jetta. We don't think he ever intended to give her back after one night, and we didn't give him the chance. The MC went in and got her out, killing the bad guy and all but one of his guards and the chef. Dev and Jetta are engaged, so are Silas and the chef. Malcolm is married to the bad guy's daughter and they have a daughter together, so it worked out for everyone in the end, but I think Nash still feels guilty because he took out more of the assholes than the rest of us combined."

I consider all of that for a while then ask, "So, Nash killed bad men to save an innocent woman."

"Yes."

"And you…"

"I did what I had to do to keep the guys safe and get Jetta out. We all knew what would happen when we decided to go into that house. It was us or them, and I'm glad it was them that died."

"Me too," I say with a sigh. "Thank you for answering honestly."

"Thank you for asking me to stay," he replies, and I can hear the smile in his voice. "I hate to move, but I need to clean up and get this rubber off."

He lets me go so that I can sit up again and he can climb out of bed. "Do you have any more condoms?"

"Yeah, why?" he asks, standing in front of me naked and not the least bit embarrassed. Not that he should be. He's built like a Roman god. "Oh, fuck," he says when he figures it out for himself and chuckles. "I'll be right back."

"And I'll be waiting."

CHAPTER SEVENTEEN

Fiasco

"You're in a good mood today," Devlin says, which is when I realize I was whistling. "Feeling better?"

"Hell yes," I reply. Sex with Joanna felt like it healed my body and soul, making me feel invincible. Sleeping with her in her bed and in my arms was the best night of my life.

"You got laid," Devlin remarks. "Who's the, um, lucky lady?"

"Joanna," I reply with a grin.

"Nash's sister Joanna?" he exclaims.

"Yeah."

"Fiasco, man, you better talk to him before you go any further down that road!"

"I don't know what the big deal is," I tell him. "It's not like they grew up together. Joanna didn't even know she was his sister until last night."

"She knows?" Devlin asks.

"Yep."

"You told her?"

"It was an accident."

"And what did Nash say about you spilling the beans and fucking his sister?" Devlin huffs.

"He doesn't know I slept with her," I admit. "And I didn't fuck her."

"So, you haven't had sex with her?"

"Oh no, we definitely had sex last night. Twice, then again this morning," I tell him with a grin.

"Then why did you say you didn't fuck her?"

"Because I didn't. She's better than that. I didn't slam her into the wall while trying to ram my dick through her body. We were in her bed and kissed almost the entire time, slow and sweet."

"Oh, Jesus Christ," Dev mutters. "You've lost your fucking mind."

"No, I think Joanna must be insane," I say with a sigh. "She knows everything there is to know about me, all of the embarrassing and bad shit, and she still wants me. I don't understand why, but I'm just really fucking happy that she does."

Joanna

"So, are you ready for some fun tomorrow night?" Casey asks when she catches up to me leaving the hospital after my shift.

"Tomorrow night?" I repeat in confusion.

"The bar in Wilmington? Hot bikers?"

"Oh, right. I don't think I'll be able to go with you," I tell her.

"Why not?"

"Because I'm not sure how Phillip would feel about me going to a biker bar trying to pick up men after sleeping with him last night."

"You what?" she exclaims as we, thankfully, escape out the back door that leads to the employee parking lot. "You slept with the big, blond biker?"

"Yes."

"Last night?"

"Uh-huh."

"And? How was it?" she asks.

"It was…really amazing."

"Yay!" Casey exclaims as she gives me a side hug. "I'm so happy you're getting out there and getting yours again."

"Yeah, but when he left this morning, he was in a hurry to get to work and didn't say he wanted to see me again. I still don't even have his phone number!"

"Don't worry. He'll be back. Now that you gave him the good shit, he won't be able to stay away."

"The good shit?" I repeat with a smile.

"If it was amazing for you, then it was probably spectacular for him," she says.

"How do you know?" I ask.

"Did he get you to the glory land?" she asks with a smirk.

My smile widens. "Yes. Several times, in fact."

"That's what I mean. Men always come when they have sex, right? If they put in the time and effort to make it good for you too, then it's even better for him, not just the sex but for his ego. He'll be back for more, I guarantee it."

"And if he doesn't?"

"He will," she says like it's a certainty.

"I hope you're right. It was more than good sex, it was nice just being so close to him, falling asleep in his arms, waking up to him kissing my neck…"

"And poking you in the ass with his morning wood?" Casey finishes.

"That too," I agree with a bark of laughter.

"Ah, to be the object of a man's desire morning, noon, and night. What more could a girl want?"

"Exactly," I agree. "And you want to see if you're still who Hunt desires?"

"That man probably has a different woman in his bed morning, noon, and night," she says with a shake of her head. "I was nothing but a little afternoon delight for him that day in your bathroom."

"Then why see him again?" I ask. "Because he got you to the glory land a few times?"

"Yes, that, and because he's a challenge. If I could make him roll over and beg me for another round, then no man would be safe from me," she says with a grin.

CHAPTER EIGHTEEN

Fiasco

As soon as I get off work, I take a quick shower and then drive over to Joanna's house. I don't let myself think about what I'm doing for too long, scared that I will talk myself out of seeing her. If she doesn't want to see me, then she won't answer the door. But after last night and this morning…well, I hope she wants to see me too.

I knock on her door and don't have to wait long before she opens it smiling, letting me inside.

"Hey," she says, looking happy to see me, happier than anyone has ever looked when I show up. Usually, it's the opposite, a worried frown like people are wondering what shit I'll fuck up.

"Hey."

We stand there just staring at each other until there's a whine from the living room.

"Is he okay?" I ask before I start walking in that direction. Ace is curled up in his bed, so I squat down and rub his head.

"He's fine," Joanna says from behind me. "Now I'm starting to wonder if you're here to see me or the dog."

That makes me chuckle as I straighten and turn to her. "I can't fuck Ace, can I?"

Once the words leave my mouth, I realize how idiotic they are. It also makes it sound like the only reason I'm here is to fuck Joanna, which isn't true.

I wait for her to get angry and throw me out. But instead, she laughs and says, "Well, I guess you could, but I'm pretty sure it's illegal and incredibly disturbing to even think about."

"I'm sorry. That was stupid," I tell her.

"I knew it was a joke. That's why I laughed," she says when she winds her arms around my waist and presses her cheek to my chest in a hug. I hold her to me as she adds, "Maybe I'm a little jealous that you came to see Ace before you gave me a hug or a kiss."

"Let me fix that right now," I tell her. Reaching for her chin, I tilt her head back and bend down to kiss her lips. She's so short and I'm so tall that it's not a very comfortable position for my back. I let go of her face that seems happy enough to keep kissing me to run both of my hands down her back and to her ass and heft her up my body while holding her upper thighs.

"Phillip!" Joanna exclaims. "Put me down! You'll hurt your side."

I didn't even feel the pain until she mentioned it, and then there's the dull ache that comes and goes while I work during the day. "I can handle it long enough to get you to the bed," I tell her.

"Your side is still healing!" she reminds me.

"Yeah, it is. So maybe tonight you can do all of the work?" I suggest.

"Deal," she agrees.

We get each other undressed in record time, and then I let Joanna make all the decisions. Having her take me in her mouth until I'm wet enough for her to ride is better than anything I could've thought up. Seeing her moving above me like a goddess makes me feel like I'm the luckiest man in the world.

Still, for a moment, I can't help but wonder what I'll eventually do to fuck it all up.

∾

Joanna

I LIE DRAPED LIMPLY over Phillip after one of the most energetic rounds of sex I've ever had. Then I remember his injured side and slide off of him gently.

"Jesus, woman," he mutters, his eyes still closed. "Last night and this morning we may have made love, but tonight you thoroughly fucked my brains out."

"Is that a compliment?" I ask with a giggle.

"Hell yes. I think I'm temporarily blind."

His hand slaps down on the side of my face and then lower where he squeezes my breast, making me squirm. "I'll have to feel my way around from now on I guess."

I laugh and scoot up the bed to kiss his lips and run my fingers through his hair as his palms roam up and down my back. "I wasn't sure if you were coming over tonight or not," I admit as we lie together.

"I wasn't sure if you wanted me to come over again tonight," he says, stroking my hair like it's a new compulsion, the same as mine.

"I'm glad you came."

"Me too," he says with a deep masculine chuckle from the double entendre.

"You know what I meant," I say with a playful slap to his chest.

"Yes, I know what you meant," he agrees.

"I don't even have your phone number."

"I don't use my phone much. It's more for just emergencies."

"Oh," I mutter, not sure if he means that or just doesn't want me to be able to call him.

"I'd rather see you in person than talk on the phone," he adds, which makes me feel better. I'm not sure why I've been feeling so insecure with Phillip. Maybe it's that I don't think he's the type of man to settle down with just one woman. He's handsome and sexy. The fact that he's a bad boy biker only adds to his appeal.

But I need to be careful, or I'll start falling for him too fast and end up getting hurt. That's why I tell him, "My friend, Casey, wants me to go to Wilmington with her tomorrow."

"Yeah? What's in Wilmington?" he asks, and it feels like he's wrapping a strand of my hair around his finger.

"A biker bar."

"There's one of those here too," he reminds me.

"Yes, but Hunt invited Casey to come see him at their bar."

"You're going to the Knights of Wrath's bar?"

"Is that what they are?" I ask, and then he's raising up on his elbow to see me better.

"They were Knights until the night I got shot. They patched over and became another Dirty Aces MC."

"That's where you were shot?" I ask since I didn't know that or don't remember if Nash or anyone else mentioned it.

"Yeah, so I don't really like the idea of you and your friend going down there."

"I thought the MC worked out everything with the group who did the shooting?"

"They did," Phillip says as he sits all the way up, which means I have to do the same. I keep the sheet pressed to my chest while he doesn't seem to notice or care that he's exposed all the way down to his bare thighs. "But that doesn't mean it's still safe. Those men are new members, and they nearly got us killed by not telling us about the threat against them!"

"You don't like Hunt and his guys," I say in understanding.

"Not really, not after what happened that night. We were blind-sided. Literally. I was…I was outside, unprotected when the shooting went down."

"I'm sorry," I tell him.

"Tell your friend not to go. If she does, she'll be putting herself in danger."

"I'm not sure if I can talk Casey out of going. The danger isn't exactly a deterrent for her…"

"What do you mean?"

"I think she's turned on by the fact that Hunt is a dangerous guy."

"Fuck," Phillip says, running his fingers through the front of his blond hair to push it back out of his face. "Then, if she wants to go, I'm going with you."

"You'll go with us?" I ask. "Even though it's the place where you nearly died?"

"The odds of anyone getting shot there again are probably low, but I would rather be there to make sure you're safe than be a pussy about it."

"You could never be a pussy," I assure him with a small smile. I let go of the sheet to straddle his hips so I can kiss him. It seems the best way to accommodate the difference in our height.

Phillip's hands grip the back of my neck and my back to hold me to him tighter as our kiss grows from sweet and gentle to something more demanding. Against my lips, he eventually says, "If I'm not careful, I think you might make me go soft."

I press my hips down on the part of him that's growing longer, thicker and harder, making him groan before I tell him, "There's nothing soft about you right now."

CHAPTER NINETEEN

Fiasco

I'm feeling a little uneasy as Joanna pulls into the parking lot of the former Knights' bar. The good thing is that I was pretty drunk that night and don't remember much about the place other than the alley where everything happened.

You can bet your ass that I'm not going anywhere near there in the dark tonight. But even worse than being nervous for myself, I'm worried about taking Joanna and her friend into such a rowdy place. They're not the usual kind of women that come to these types of bars looking for a good time, a few free drinks, and a quick fuck.

At least I didn't think they were, but then when Joanna and Casey get out of the car, it's a reminder that they're not exactly dressed like conservative nurses. Joanna's black dress is short and tight in all the right places. The swell of her tits is almost spilling out of the top, and fuck, I want to take a bite out of them. At least the rest of her is covered. I didn't really mean to look; but when Casey got out of the backseat of Joanna's car on the same side as me, I saw a flash of her red thong. Even standing up, her skirt is so short her ass cheeks are hanging out the bottom. Then there's her top, which doesn't have enough material to even be considered a shirt. It's more like a black spandex bra that covers her nipples and leaves her entire stomach bare, yet is so thin you can see every inch of those hard points, which reminds me of Joanna's satin nightie she was wearing the first time we were together.

Joanna clears her throat from beside me in what sounds like a warning. I look at her face that's frowning and then to Casey's smiling one where she looks way too pleased with herself.

"She's begging to get fucked six ways from Sunday," I say to Joanna in my defense.

"Yes, I am," Casey agrees before she starts strutting toward the door of the bar in her sky-high heels.

"Do you need a towel to wipe the drool off your mouth?" Joanna asks as we stay standing next to her car in the dark lot.

"I wasn't checking her out," I tell her.

"Uh-huh."

Grabbing her hand, I put it on my dick to prove that I wasn't thinking about screwing her friend. While holding it there, I bend down and lick a line down the center of her chest and flick my tongue around that dip of her cleavage like I'm licking something else lower. That's when my cock finally gives a twitch of interest.

"Phillip!" Joanna moans my name like she has for me the last few nights. I'd rather be at her house in her bed than getting ready to go into a bar with a bunch of guys.

"Are you two coming inside or planning to just come right out here?" Casey calls out.

"We-we're coming!" Joanna responds, so I remove my hand from hers that's on my dick. She doesn't immediately let go, though. Her fingers tighten and give me a squeeze through my jeans that makes me groan as my knees go weak. "Later?" she asks.

"Oh yeah," I agree. Removing her hand from me before I haul her into the backseat of her car, I intertwine her fingers with mine without even thinking about it. I'm not sure if I've ever held hands with a woman before. But, with Joanna, it just feels right.

"I'm going inside!" Casey tells us before she opens the door and walks into the bar.

"I hope she doesn't get more than she bargained for later," I tell Joanna as we start crossing the parking lot hand in hand.

"She came here looking to have dirty sex with Hunt," Joanna tells me. "They've hooked up before."

"Oh yeah?"

"Yeah. At my house while you were still recovering."

"From what I heard from the club girls that hang around here, if you fuck one of the members of the Knights, you fuck them all."

"That can't be true," Joanna says.

"That's what I was told by two of them. I don't think a gang bang is something any woman would lie about."

"Maybe they were just trying to shock you."

"Maybe," I agree, giving her hand a squeeze before I open the door with my other hand and hold it open for her to go inside first.

Just as I remember, it's a rough little bar with loud music playing, smoke billowing up from cigarettes and joints. There are more men than women here at the moment. All of them are either looking at Casey or Joanna because they're by far the freshest meat. Casey might be dressed like an easy layup tonight, but Joanna just looks like a beautiful woman. Any man would be damn lucky to get to lay a finger on her.

She's the first woman I've ever wanted to keep by my side to make sure no one else even thinks about touching her.

I've never been jealous before. Like the rumors about the old Knights, in the past, I could've shared a woman with every man in the room and not have cared what they did to her as long as the sex was good when I got a turn.

But with Joanna, I feel like she's mine. I don't want to share her with any other man, not even in their wettest dreams.

～

Joanna

THE BAR IS a little trashier than I expected, and my expectations were already low. While the number of men with tattoos and beards easily outnumber women at least three to one, two girls appear out of thin air and come right for Phillip, eyeing him like he's their favorite toy even with my hand in his.

"Fiasco!" one of them exclaims. "Only you could take two bullets and show up here a few weeks later, still looking like an Adonis."

"You know I don't know what the fuck an Adonis is, Crystal," Phillip tells her with a smile when she hugs up on him right on his injured side. That bothers me more than anything, even the fact that he knows her name.

"I hate we didn't get to finish that night together," the other woman says when she runs her claws down the center of his chest. She probably would've gone lower if Phillip hadn't grabbed her hand to stop her.

Instead of talking more about the 'night they didn't get to finish together,' Phillip introduces us. "Wanda, Crystal, this is my girlfriend, Joanna."

"Girlfriend?" the women both say in surprise, echoing the voice in my head. Did he really just call me his girlfriend? Maybe he's just trying to get rid of the handsy women.

"Joanna saved my life after I got shot. If not for her, I wouldn't be standing here tonight," Phillip says as he smiles down at me so warmly it feels like the sun is shining on me.

"Then we need to buy her a drink!" one of them says as she grabs my arm and pulls me to the bar while the one with claws stands in front of Phillip, blocking his way so that I have to let his hand go.

"Bernard, give this woman the strongest drink you can make," she tells him, pulling a ten out of her cleavage and slapping it on the bar.

"Coming right up," the man agrees.

"Thanks, I guess," I tell her. I look over my shoulder to where several men have joined the other woman so that Phillip is so surrounded by well-wishers that I can only see the top of his blond head.

"Fiasco is amazing, isn't he?" she asks me.

"Uh-huh."

"Not the brightest bulb in the box, but he knows how to use his tongue and dick."

"Yes, he does," I agree through clenched teeth.

When the bartender places some kind of drink in front of me, I stare at it and consider guzzling it down. But at the moment, I would rather leave this place. If I drink, I can't drive myself home.

Casey comes up on the other side of me and sighs. "I need a drink or ten. There's no sign of Hunt yet."

"Help yourself," I tell her, reaching for the glass and sliding it to her.

"Bitch," the woman on the other side of me hisses before she disappears.

"Well, they're giving us a warm welcome, aren't they?" Casey asks as she guzzles the drink.

"I think she's pissed that Phillip called me his girlfriend."

"His girlfriend? Really? That's hilarious."

"Why is it hilarious?" I ask.

"Because it sounds so junior high," Casey replies with a grin.

"I think it's sweet."

"It is, but do you really think he means it?"

"I don't think he would've said it if he didn't mean it," I respond defensively.

Casey shrugs and then drinks the rest of the mixed drink. She's just slammed the glass down and asked the bartender for another one when a deep, growly voice says, "Well, I'll be dammed." A man's hands come around to grab her tits possessively, and then I hear him whisper into her ear, "Who let a naughty little nurse in here tonight?"

"Hunt!" Casey exclaims, then pushes his hands away so she can spin around to face him. That's when I finally take in his face that's familiar since he was one of our other patients from the shooting.

His golden hair is thick and long enough that there are waves in it, but it's not falling into his eyes like Phillip's does sometimes. He's a ruggedly handsome guy with several days' worth of stubble on his strong jaw. And while he's not quite as tall and thick as Phillip, he looks like a man who is strong as an ox, not the kind of strength that you get from working out in a gym for vanity's sake. Then there are his eyes that are so dark they're nearly black and full of the promise of all sorts of naughty things.

"What?" Hunt asks Casey not so innocently. "We both know why you came here tonight, don't we, darlin'?"

Well, he's right about that. She came with the hope of getting naked with him. He must be talented for her to go all out tonight. I can see what Phillip meant about Casey dressing to get fucked. She's barely covered her boobs and ass, making her look like a walking invitation asking for more of what Hunt and she did in my bathroom together that day. Loudly.

Instead of admitting the reason she came tonight, Casey says, "I'm here with my friend, Joanna, just having a few drinks." She glances at me and laughs at what is probably a shocked look on my face, not looking the least bit bothered by him grabbing her breasts like he owned them.

Hunt eyes me too for a second before his attention returns to Casey, then he runs his tongue seductively over his bottom lip. "Both of you mine to play with tonight, or are you just going to tease my dick with a little girl-on-girl action?"

Oh heck no.

"I'm not feeling too well," I blurt out in a rush as I search the crowd for Phillip. "I think I'll ask Fiasco to take me home," I say, using his nickname since that's probably the only name Hunt knows he goes by.

"You're no fun," Casey tells me with a fake pout. I know her; and even if I wasn't seeing Phillip, she would want Hunt all to herself. She's welcome to him since he looks like a man who could get a little too rough in bed.

"I'll, ah, call you tomorrow," I say when I slip off the stool to search for Fiasco.

I find him talking to two men in the same leather MC cuts while a woman's hand from behind tries to slide underneath his shirt. He pulls her wrist away and is still holding it when her other hand starts trying to do the exact same thing on the other side.

That's the moment that Phillip looks up and locks eyes with me, freezing while holding the other woman's wrist in each of his hands.

"I'm leaving," I tell him loud enough that he can hear over the music or read my lips when I start to the door.

"Joanna!" he calls out, but I don't stop.

This place is insane! Do people only come here to get drunk and have sex with each other? "Joanna!" Phillip says again before I escape out the door.

I drink in the cool night air that feels good on my arms and legs since my skin is overheating from anger or from how awkward I felt inside.

"Joanna, wait!" Phillip says when he jogs to catch up with me just as another man's voice says, "Everything okay out here?"

"We're fine, Preston. Go back inside," Phillip answers without turning around, like he knows the man.

"Hunt didn't want her out here alone."

"I'm with her. And if she's leaving, then I am too."

"Okay, man. Good to see you healthy," Preston says before he goes back inside.

"Are you sure you want to leave? I thought you might want to stay and catch up with your old friends!"

"I only came tonight because you and Casey insisted on coming, remember?" he says, which has some of my anger deflating out of me.

Still, the women in the bar, the ones hanging all over him, are just the reminder I needed that I shouldn't be so quick to trust him or care about him after just a few nights together. I need space, distance, before I lose more of myself to him than I should.

I hurry to get my keys out of my purse; but before I can open the driver door, Phillip is suddenly there, blocking it with his much bigger body.

"Is Casey ready to leave too?" he asks me.

"No."

"And you're just going to leave her here with no way home?"

"Casey's a grown woman. She knew what she was getting into when she decided to come," I tell him, annoyed with her and with Phillip. "Did you sleep with those women who came up to you?"

"Yes," he answers immediately. "The night I got shot. I was actually fucking one of them when I got shot."

"Oh."

I had expected him to deny it, not admit to everything and share so much information.

"But I barely remember anything but their names," he goes on to add. "We were drinking and having fun until the shooting started. I was only one of two of the original Aces that was single."

"Really?" I say in surprise. "The others have serious relationships?"

"Yep."

"Serious enough that they don't sleep around?"

"Hardly any girls even come around the pool hall or the gambling cruise anymore because they're all settled down hard. It was one of the reasons I was glad to come over here for a party a few weeks ago with a bunch of women who actually wanted to fuck me."

Again, that's more honesty from him than I expected.

"You don't have to leave with me if you don't want to, Phillip," I tell him.

"Did you hear what I said in there?" he asks as he places both of his hands gently on my hips. "I told them you're my girlfriend, and I meant that. At least that's how I feel about you, even if you just see me as a fuck buddy."

"I don't think of you as a fuck buddy. How could you say that?" I ask him.

"Because that's all I've ever been to any woman."

"That's sort of sad," I tell him.

He shrugs. "It's true. I'm good at fucking and that's about it."

"I liked being with you before we ever slept together," I remind him.

"Yeah?" he asks with a smile that glows in the night.

"Yes. But I should also confess that I did kiss you when you were recovering."

"I knew it!" he exclaims, his fingers tightening on my waist. "I woke up feeling your lips on my forehead, my cheek, then my lips."

I lower my eyes in shame. "I'm sorry. I shouldn't have done that, but you were just so...handsome, and I wanted you to wake up and get better."

His arms wrap around my back, and then he dips down all that height so that his lips are suddenly buried in my neck as I rest my chin on his shoulder and pull him even closer.

We hold each other like that for a long time, until Phillip breaks the silence. His words are muffled since he doesn't try to pull away. "Will you come with me Sunday?"

"Sunday?" I repeat.

"I want you to meet Sierra and Asher."

"If you're sure?"

"I'm sure," he says, finally pulling back to look down at me.

"I love kids," I admit to him.

"Yeah?"

"Yes."

"Most women wouldn't want to date me because I have two kids with two different women."

"Then most women are stupid," I tell him with a smile.

CHAPTER TWENTY

Fiasco

"I hope the women don't give you any grief," I tell Joanna as she drives us to the playground.

"Why would they?" she asks.

"That's just how they are. Don't take it personally if they do, okay?"

"Okay," she agrees.

God, she's so easygoing no matter what, which is not something I'm used to from the women I sleep with. Most are demanding as shit, especially Katrina and Giselle, the mothers of my kids. They don't make anything easy, and I always feel like it's a huge burden on them to meet me every Sunday afternoon at two for an hour.

"I'm pretty fucking lucky they agree to give me one hour a week," I grumble aloud.

I didn't say that they only conceded that time because it's when I bring them money. I'm not stupid, but I know it's what Joanna is thinking too when she frowns while she watches the road.

"Would you like to see more of them?" she asks, stealing a quick glance at me.

"I've tried, but they won't budge. Besides, they have their own lives. I can't ask them to take more time out of it to babysit me with them."

"You're their father. They don't need to babysit you with them, Phillip."

"That's not what they think."

"Forget the mothers. Do *you* want more time with your son and daughter?" Joanna asks more sternly.

"Of course I do, but it's a lost cause. Trust me, angel, I've tried."

"I'm not promising anything, but maybe I could help you when you have them, not because you need my help, but because I would like to help."

"Really?" I ask. "You haven't even met them yet. You might think they're annoying little brats." I think they're the sweetest two people to ever walk the earth, but I could be biased since they're mine.

"I doubt that," she says with a smile.

"Then, yes, I would like to have more time with them and with you."

"So, if I have a chance today, would you let me try to talk to them for you?" Joanna asks.

She glances over, and I give her a smile before she looks back at the road. Needing to touch her, even though it's only been a few minutes since the last time, I reach over and place my palm on her closest knee to give it a squeeze. "I would let you do anything you asked, angel."

"Anything?" she repeats with her own teasing grin.

"Yep. Anything, even put a finger in my ass, and my ass is usually off limits to everyone."

Joanna laughs out loud, and it's one of the most beautiful sounds in the world. And I know she's not laughing at me like most people do. For some unknown reason, she actually thinks I'm funny.

"Your ass is safe from me. I promise."

"I really love being with you, Joanna," I tell her honestly and give her leg another squeeze. "You make me feel really damn good, like maybe I'm not a complete waste of space like everyone's told me my whole life."

"Oh, Phillip," she says sadly, covering my hand on her leg and driving with one hand on the steering wheel. "That's not true. You are a strong, kind, loyal, hardworking, handsome, and incredibly sexy man. Don't let anyone let you think otherwise."

And for the first time in my life, I start to think maybe she's right and the rest of the world is wrong.

~

Joanna

WHEN FIASCO and I pull up to the park on Sunday, I can immediately see his two children running around on the playground. Their blond hair is shining in the sunlight, the same way their father seems to always glow angelically. As we begin to cross the grass, the children come running over to greet us, both of them overjoyed at the sight of their dad.

Asher and Sierra stand still for about two seconds while Phillip introduces me to them, and then they're off, running full out and screaming like a horde of zombies are chasing them as Phillip sprints behind the young pair.

I glance over at the bench where their mothers are sitting. Both of them are scrolling on their cell phones, intentionally not looking at me or Phillip. I guess this is the usual Sunday play date, since the kids and Fiasco seem unperturbed.

When I walk over, I tell them, "He's really good with them, the kids." They may be sitting on the same bench, but they are as far apart as they can get. I'm guessing they're not exactly friends.

"Yeah, because he's just a big kid himself," the one on the right says with a grin. I believe Phillip said her name was Giselle. She's tall and lean with long strawberry blonde hair that I think may be natural since she's Sierra's mother and they look so much alike. Her model-like beauty makes me feel a little insecure. At least she's not dressed for the runway this afternoon. Instead, she's wearing a pair of black yoga pants and a plain white t-shirt with sneakers.

"I'm glad to get a chance to meet you all," I say in the silence that follows. "I don't know how much Phillip told you about me…"

"Phillip?" the mother on the left says in confusion — Katrina, if I remember right. She's shorter and curvier than Giselle and me both, almost on the overweight size with burgundy hair that can't be natural curled in soft waves. She's not as pretty as Giselle, but I'm guessing men wouldn't care because of her other attributes spilling out of her V-neck top and filling out the back of her skinny jeans.

I point my finger at the man running around the swing set with his daughter now on his shoulders, chasing his son. "He's the father of your children, and you don't even know his real name?" I say in disbelief. Then a thought hits me. "Didn't you put his name on the birth certificate?"

"No," both of them say at the same time, which is odd.

"Has he ever taken a DNA test?"

That earns me two very similar glares. "Who the fuck do you think you are, showing up here and sticking your nose in our business?" Katrina asks while sweeping her hair back over her shoulder.

"Calm down, Trina," Giselle says softly. To me, she says, "Yes, we both have had DNA tests done, but nothing was ever formalized. Court shit is expensive, and Fiasco has always been good about paying us every week."

"Except lately," Katrina mutters as she eyes me like it's my fault he's not giving her every penny he has.

"Have either of you ever been to Phillip's apartment?"

They both shake their heads no.

"He gives everything he has to those two kids and barely keeps enough to buy himself food or pay rent. And the reason he hasn't been earning as much lately is because he was out of work recovering from two gunshot wounds! Speaking as the nurse who saved him, he should've been out at least six weeks or more, but he went back to work sooner than he should have. He could have killed himself going back so early, but hey, he's here with the money, right?"

"You're a nurse?" Giselle asks.

"Yes," I answer, forcing myself to calm down. Yelling at them won't get them to like me. "I work at Masonboro General. I love children; and even though I haven't known Phillip long, I care about him a great deal. If you would both agree, we would really like to have Asher and Sierra over to my house for a playdate one afternoon."

"I don't think so," Katrina says while Giselle silently considers it.

"You could come over beforehand and inspect my place, make sure it's kid safe. I can show you my credentials from the hospital. I'm sure you both have a ton of things to do or could just use the time alone for yourself. Think of it as a free babysitter for a few hours."

"I'm in," Giselle agrees with a smile. "Tell us when and where."

"You don't speak for me," Katrina huffs.

"Oh, come off it, Trina. Joanna and…Phillip are just as trustworthy as the teenager you let stay with Asher while you go out on dates."

"Can you watch him one night while I go out?" Katrina asks me.

"Of course. And maybe once you feel comfortable with them coming over to play, they could have sleepovers."

"Girl, do you know the last morning I slept past seven?" Giselle asks, and I shake my head with an answering grin. "Before Sierra was born!"

"Asher sleeps until eight," Katrina says. "But never a minute later."

"Then a sleepover is something we can all hopefully look forward to in the future."

"I don't think Fiasco…Phillip has ever had a girlfriend before," Giselle tells me.

"I know. That's a shame."

"I never expected him to end up with someone like you," Katrina mutters, and I'm not sure if that's an insult or a compliment. Giselle just looks at me and rolls her eyes with a smile, so I don't think too hard about what the other woman thinks about me.

CHAPTER TWENTY-ONE

Fiasco

"Thank you so much for doing this," I tell Joanna as I wrap my arms around her, trapping her arms by her side to kiss her cheek from behind.

"It's the least I can do," she says. "As much money as you pay in child support, you should get to see them whenever you want."

"Katrina and Giselle wouldn't agree to that, but I'm happy that they are letting them come to your place and play for a few hours. I don't think they would leave them with me if they saw my apartment."

"How is it that neither of them know where you live or your real name?" she asks.

I let go of her arms to spin her around to face me, then place my hands on her hips to pull her closer. "Have you ever had a one-night stand?"

"No," she responds and looks embarrassed.

"I didn't think so. And that's not a bad thing. I just meant that first names are about as much information as you get before you fuck someone. If Giselle and Katrina hadn't gotten pregnant, I probably wouldn't have seen either of them again. And nobody uses my real name except for you."

"Not even your family?"

"Especially not my family," I agree.

"That's just sad."

"I've gotten used to Fiasco," I say with a shrug. "But I'm glad you call me Phillip."

"I'll try to break others of calling you Fiasco too."

"You don't have to do that, angel. They only know me as Fiasco, and that's what I'll always be to them."

"Fine," she says with a sigh. "But if it bothers you, you should tell them to stop, even if they're your friends or family."

"I'll think about it," I assure her.

"Good." She leans in for a quick kiss and then says, "Now, I need to get Ace and his things moved to the bedroom before they get here."

"What? Why can't he stay in the living room? The kids will love him," I tell her.

"Because they're kids, and Ace is a stray. Until we know how he acts around strangers and kids, we shouldn't let them play together."

"He'll be fine with them. I've never met a sweeter dog…" I say but realize that's a lie. "Well, I have, but that was a long time ago."

"The puppy your mom's boyfriend killed?" Joanna asks, and I nod as I swallow around the knot in my throat that's always there when I think of how I couldn't save Rosie or her puppies.

"What he did was incredibly cruel, and I'm so sorry."

"Me too," I agree just as I hear a knock on the door. "They're here!"

"Give me a hand with Ace?" Joanna asks.

I bend down and scoop him and his bed up in my arms. "I'll take him to your bedroom and come back for his food and water if you want to get the door?"

∼

Joanna

SIERRA AND ASHER love playing with the new Legos Phillip and I picked up yesterday for their visit along with a few coloring books. If we're going to make this a recurring event, then we'll need to have even more toys on hand. And I do hope they get to come back. I can see how happy Phillip is to be with them. Seeing him happy makes me happy too. Besides, his son and daughter are at that incredibly sweet age before they learn to talk back or be mean. They're actually sweet to each other.

"I hear a doggie!" Sierra says when Ace lets out a bark from the bedroom.

"He must need to go outside," I tell Phillip as I get to my feet.

"You want me to take him?"

"No, you stay with the kids, and I'll be right back."

I get Ace's leash from the wall next to the back door and take it to put on him, then sneak out that way before the kids can see him. Phillip is right, Ace is a sweet dog, but we don't know the type of home he came from. Some animals don't do well with children.

When we come back inside, though, both kids come running. "Can we see the doggie?" Asher asks.

"Wow," Sierra says as she looks up at Ace with bright, excited eyes.

"Sorry, they heard you come back inside and wanted to see him," Phillip says with a wince.

"Okay," I say with a sigh. "But you have to be gentle with him, okay?"

"Okay," the kids both agree.

I sit down on the sofa with Ace taking up all of my lap so they can pet his head. His tail starts wagging like crazy, and then he's trying to give them kisses. Both Sierra and Asher squeal happily, and then Ace tries to jump to the floor. I lower him down gently so he can keep the weight off of his bad leg.

"What happened to his leg?" Asher asks, kneeling down next to him.

"He had a little accident," Phillip explains.

I start to warn them not to touch the cast, but I'm too late. Asher grabs it, making Ace whine and then growl before he turns around and snaps at the boy.

"Ace!" Phillip exclaims. He scoops Sierra up in his arms while Asher starts to cry. Since I'm closest to Asher, I pick him up. His eyes are closed tight, tears racing down his cheeks as he starts to wail.

"It's okay, Asher," I tell him. "You just startled him, and he made a noise to warn you, that's all."

He shakes his head back and forth then holds up his tiny hand. "He bit me!"

My heart drops as I hurry him down the hallway to the bathroom where I keep the first aid kit. When I sit him down on the closed toilet to take his hand and examine it, I expect to see blood, but thankfully it's just a couple of teeth indentions. Ace did bite him, but it didn't break the skin.

"Shh, it's okay," I tell the still squalling child. "We'll get you some ice, and your hand will be as good as new. You don't even need a band-aid."

That has him pausing in his howling. He blinks his big, brown eyes at me, lashes darkened by tears and says, "I don't?"

"Nope."

For some reason, that makes his lip quiver, and then the crying starts up again even louder.

"How bad is it?" Phillip asks from the doorway, still holding Sierra in a near death-grip. The little girl doesn't seem to mind. Her arms are around his neck, holding on as tight she can with her head resting on his shoulder.

"Just a few indentions, but the teeth didn't break the skin," I tell him.

"Thank fu-God," he mutters, catching the swear word just in time.

"Does it hurt, buddy?" Phillip asks Asher, who nods vehemently.

"I told him he didn't even need a band-aid and that made him start crying again," I explain.

"He likes band-aids," Sierra tells us calmly. "Especially ones with the Avengers on them."

"Is that what you want?" I kneel in front of Asher and ask him. Grabbing some toilet paper, I start to dry his face. "Do you want us to get you an Avengers band-aid?"

He nods his head, and his crying finally begins to calm down. "Avengers make it all better," Asher says.

"I can run to the store," Phillip says.

"Okay." I look up at him and give him a small smile, but he looks as pissed as I've ever seen him for some reason. "Are you okay, Phillip?" I ask, and he nods without giving a verbal response. "Well, how about you let Miss Sierra stay in here with us while you get Ace back into his comfy bed in the bedroom?"

Phillip places a kiss on her forehead and then lowers her to her feet in the bathroom. Sierra comes over and takes her half-brother's injured hand, lifting it to her lips to kiss it.

"Does it feel better now?" she asks Asher, and he nods.

It's one of the sweetest interactions between siblings that I've ever seen. That's when I realize that Phillip isn't the only one suffering seeing his son and daughter for just one hour a week. Asher and Sierra obviously enjoy being together. I didn't notice on the playground, but it's been clear this afternoon that they play really well together, no arguing or fussing, just sharing and enjoying their time together like good friends.

I glance over to see if Phillip was as moved by them as I was but barely catch a glimpse of his back as he leaves. The bedroom door closes a moment later, and then I hear him go out the front door.

"How about a snack and a juice box while we wait for Daddy to get back?" I ask the kids, who both smile.

By the time Phillip returns with the requested band-aids, Sierra and Asher are back to playing with their Lego blocks like nothing happened.

Phillip sits down and asks to see Asher's hand, turning it this way and that to assess the damage. Then, finally, he places the bandage over it.

"He's been fine," I tell him softly when I sit down next to him and rub his arm.

"He's not fine," Phillip whispers to me. "His mama is going to have my balls for this."

"What do you mean? The teeth indentions are already fading. There's barely a mark on him."

"She'll still blame me," he says.

"He grabbed an injured dog's leg, and the dog reacted. It's not your fault, Phillip. Just an unfortunate accident."

"It could've been a lot worse," he says, his jaw clenched tight as he watches the kids play. "You told me not to let them around the dog, and I didn't listen."

"Now we know. I'm sure Ace will be fine to play with them once his leg is all healed."

Phillip shakes his head but doesn't comment.

In fact, he doesn't say much to me the rest of the night, mostly playing with Asher and Sierra.

When there's a knock on the door, Phillip jumps as if he's been struck.

"It's going to be okay," I tell him as we both get up from the floor to answer the door. "We'll just explain to them what happened. I'm sure they'll understand."

"No, they won't," he grumbles as he stands there and waits for me to open the door.

"Hey! How did it go?" Giselle asks. "Did Sierra behave?"

"Sierra was great," I tell her. "She's so sweet to her brother."

"Yeah, they've always got along great since they're only a few months apart." She smiles at me and then looks to Phillip, who still looks angry. "What's wrong, Fiasco?" she asks, her brow furrowed, calling him by the awful nickname again.

"I may as well tell you because I know Katrina will if I don't," he says. Taking a deep breath, he launches into the story. "Ace bit Asher.

It didn't break the skin, but he hurt him, and he cried bloody murder for a while."

"He's fine," I reiterate. "Just left a few teeth marks, but he didn't bleed or bruise."

"Who is Ace?" Giselle asks me.

"Our...my dog. I haven't had him long. He's a stray that I took in after an accident that hurt his leg. That's the only reason why he snapped at Asher."

Her face turns a bright, bright shade of red. "You have a wild dog and didn't think to tell me that when I dropped off my daughter? What if he had taken a bite out of Asher's face or Sierra's?" She pushes past me, going over to scoop Sierra up in her arms, propping her on her hip.

"We didn't intend to let Ace near the kids. I took him outside; and when we came back, the kids saw him and wanted to pet him."

"Well, you should've watched him better!" she yells at us before she turns her attention to Sierra, making sure she doesn't have any injuries.

Shit. If Giselle is this upset when the bite didn't even happen to her kid, then Katrina is going to go nuts. She may very well physically hurt us.

Unfortunately, we aren't able to calm Giselle down and convince her to leave before Katrina comes waltzing into the open door without knocking.

"What's going on?" she asks, picking up on the tension in the room.

"They have a psycho dog that bit Asher!" Giselle tells the other woman before we can tell her calmly.

"What?" she exclaims and then hurries over to kneel in front of Asher, pulling him to his feet.

"I got a boo boo, but Daddy got the Avengers band-aids, so I'm all better now."

Katrina yanks the bandage off so fast that Asher starts crying again. "There are teeth marks in my son's hand!"

"Ace has a broken leg in a cast, and Asher touched it…" I start to explain, and then Katrina is on her feet and getting in my face.

"Are you saying this is all Asher's fault?" she yells at me.

"No, of course not."

"That's right. It's your fault and *his*," she says, pointing her finger at Phillip. "If you had told me about the rabid dog, I wouldn't have let my son stay here with you!"

"I'm sorry Asher got bit, but Ace really is a good dog," I assure her.

"Come on, Asher," Katrina calls to her son through gritted teeth. Asher comes over and takes her hand. "Tell Daddy goodbye, because this is the last time you'll ever see him!"

"What?" I gasp and look to Phillip, who drops to his knees and hugs Asher like he may never get to do it again. "You can't mean that," I say to Katrina. "It was an accident, and Asher is fine."

"This time maybe. There won't be a second time!" she shouts at me, her face enraged.

Sierra runs over to join her father and brother. Phillip opens his arm to bring her in for a group hug, holding her tight.

"Giselle…" I start since she's the much more sensible mother.

"No," she grits out. "Let's go, Sierra."

"Come on, Asher."

The little boy and girl run to their mothers when called like good children, and out the door they go, leaving Phillip on his knees, tears glistening on his face.

"God, Phillip, I am so sorry this happened," I tell him. "They'll probably cool off in a few days…"

"No, they won't," he says when he pulls the collar of his t-shirt, hiding his face as he dries it. "They won't ever let me see them again."

"That's not true. They can't stay upset about this forever. You're paying child support, so they have to let you see them."

"I knew this was a bad fucking idea!" he exclaims, raising his voice like I've never heard him do before as he stands up. "You asked too much of me, Joanna, and now I have nothing!"

"I'm sorry. We'll figure this out, I promise."

"You can't promise that, not after you ruined everything," he says without looking at me. He then walks out the door without another word.

I want to chase him down and beg him to forgive me, but I know it won't do any good. He's angry and hurt, and he's right — it's all my fault.

It was my idea to have the kids come to my place for the playdate. I was responsible for keeping them safe. Now, Phillip doesn't think he'll be able to see them again. He's heartbroken, like any good father would be. And now that I may have lost him, my heart is breaking right along with his.

CHAPTER TWENTY-TWO

Fiasco

I walk into the pool hall and go right behind the bar to pour a shot of Captain Morgan and throw it back with the bottle still in my hand. That little bit of rum doesn't even begin to help ease the ache inside of my chest, so I just go right to the source, pouring the amber liquid straight down my throat. I guzzle it as I make my way around the bar to climb up on one of the stools.

I'm halfway through the bottle when Nash and Malcolm come up on either side of me.

"Go easy," Malcolm says.

"You okay, man?" Nash asks, and I shake my head.

The bottle eventually runs dry, which pisses me off even more. Before I even think about it, the glass is flying over the bar and shattering against the wall.

"Jesus," someone says.

I cross my arms on the bar counter to bury my face in them.

"Get the women out of here!" Malcolm says.

"Fiasco, man. What happened?" Devlin asks, clasping his hand on my shoulder. The attempt at comforting me pisses me off, because I don't want to cry like a pussy again. Anger is better. I roll my shoulders to shrug him off and get to my feet, stumbling a little as I come off the stool because the alcohol finally is starting to take effect. Good, I want to drink until I pass out and can't think. To do that, I probably need another bottle.

The first face I see when the room stops spinning is Nash's, reminding me of his beautiful sister. "This is your fucking fault!" I say while poking him in the chest with my finger hard enough that he moves backward.

"My fault?" he asks, brown eyes like hers widening in surprise. "What the hell did I do?"

"I wish I had died rather than met your sister!"

His face falls and he says, "Fiasco, man, you don't really mean that."

"The hell I don't!" I yell in his face. "And my name is Phillip! Now get the fuck out of my way before I knock your ass out!"

"You're not going to knock anyone out," Malcolm grumbles from behind me.

Hands grab me from the side and behind to jerk me down so that I'm sitting on a stool again. "Sit down and tell us what happened," Silas says.

"What happened? What happened is that I was a stupid fucking fool for thinking Joanna knew a goddamn thing about me. She was wrong. Now, I probably won't ever see my kids again!"

"Something happened with your kids?" Devlin asks. Of all the guys, he knows me best since we work together and talk every day.

"Yes," I answer with a loud belch following not so far behind. "I hit a dog on my bike and nearly killed it. Then Joanna paid a shit ton of money to save the dog. Wouldn't you fucking know, the dog I nearly killed just bit Asher! Screw it. Keep calling me Fiasco. I don't deserve any other name. I fuck up everything I touch."

"Damn, man," someone says.

"Did you get into an argument with Joanna?" Devlin asks.

"We're done. I lost my kids and my girlfriend in one night."

"Girlfriend?" Nash asks. "You're serious about Joanna?"

"It's done and over now, so no need to get pissed at me!"

"I knew you were seeing her, but I didn't tell you to stop, did I?" Nash asks.

"Not to my face, no. I wouldn't have even if you had told me to."

"I don't care if you date Joanna. She may be my biological sister, but I don't get to have a say in her life. I didn't want her to get caught up in any of the MC's shit, but otherwise I'm not going to try and tell her or you who you can or can't see."

"Didn't you hear me?" I ask his now two identical heads that look like Joanna. "It's done. I can fuck whoever I want and make more kids."

"You don't mean that," Malcolm says. "And even if you do mean it right now, you'll hate yourself if you screw anyone else."

"I already hate myself," I mutter. "I need more rum." I try to get to my feet, but hands push me down so hard I nearly fall off the stool.

"No more alcohol. We're not going to stand around and watch you drink yourself to death," Devlin says.

"Let's get him up to the apartment upstairs. There's still a bed. He can crash there tonight and sleep this shit off," Malcolm says.

Sleep sounds like a great idea, as long as it's a dreamless one. I don't want happy dreams like ones where I'm with Joanna and she becomes a stepmother to Asher and Sierra. Nope. It'll only make me sad, and I don't think I can handle any more sadness.

Joanna

"I'M SO SORRY, BUDDY," I say to Ace as I lie on the floor of my bedroom with him, tears streaming down my face. "It wasn't your fault. It was mine. Phillip was right. I shouldn't have pushed him."

Ace lays his snout on my arm as if trying to comfort me.

"You're a good, sweet dog," I tell him, not planning to move for the rest of the night. I'll just sleep on the floor, like a mutt. I don't deserve to be comfortable, not after all the pain I've caused Phillip.

A sudden loud knock sounds at the door, and I scramble to my feet, hoping it's Phillip.

I rush to the living room. And when I open the main door, there's a man on the other side of the glass in a Dirty Aces cut and jeans, but it's not the one I wanted to see.

"Go away, Nash. I don't want to talk to you right now," I say when I start to close the door on him. But lightning fast, he opens the glass door and pushes his way in past me.

"Too bad. We need to talk."

"Get out or I'll…I'll call the police."

He stares at me coolly as if he knows I'm full of shit without commenting on that blatant lie.

"What do you want? It's late." I cross my arms over my chest to show my annoyance at his visit.

"First, I wanted to come over and apologize for not telling you the truth about us when we first met. I know it sounds stupid to say I was worried that you would throw us out, but put yourself in my shoes for a second and think about it. Would you have taken the chance of being honest while your friend was dying from two bullet wounds?"

I know he means Phillip, and now that I know him, even if it hasn't been for long, I would do anything to keep him alive.

"Fine. You're forgiven. Now, please leave."

"I know I'm not exactly the ideal brother, and I never will be. I've killed people, and I would do it again. I can't pretend I'm a good guy, but I am glad that I finally got to meet you. It's nice to know that there may be some good in me, in our mother and father, because you turned out pretty well."

"Phillip told me why you killed people. It was for a good reason," I admit.

"Good reason or not, I took lives, took people from their friends and family. They may not have been decent, but the families were."

"The fact that you can understand that means you're not as bad a person as you think you are. Unlike you, I didn't grow up in the foster system. I was lucky to have good, adoptive parents, but they're dead now, so I'm an orphan yet again."

"I'm sorry," Nash says. "Guess I'm all you've got as far as family goes."

"Guess so."

"Then, as your brother, tell me what happened with Fiasco…with *Phillip* tonight and what we can do to fix it."

"How do you know something happened?" I ask.

"Because Fi-Phillip came to the pool hall. I've never seen him so upset."

"Well, he may have just lost what little visitation he has with his son and daughter because of me. He has a right to be upset."

"I didn't know he even saw his kids."

"Once a week, every week. And he always gives both mothers everything he can from his paycheck to help out financially."

"Really?" Nash says in surprise.

"Really. He loves them so much. And now…" I shake my head and swipe the tears from under my eyes. "You and I know how much it hurts to find out your parents aren't around and didn't want us. It would be so wrong for his children to ever think that for even a second!"

"He's a good father?"

"He is," I say with a smile as more tears fall. "He cares about them and loves them more than anything, but he doesn't think that he's capable of being a father to them without supervision. And now, because of me, their mothers don't think he is either."

"Jeez, that sounds awful," Nash says, and then he's wrapping his arms around me and holding me as I cry.

When the tears finally begin to lessen, I take a deep breath and push Nash away. "Thanks, but I'm not the one who needs comforting."

"Of course you do. You care about Fi-Phillip, and you don't want him to be unhappy."

"I think I love him," I admit honestly.

"You do?"

"Yes."

"Then we need to figure out how to fix this shit so that you two can be together, because I think he loves you too."

"Really?"

Nash nods. "He's never been so upset, especially about a woman. But tonight…it was like he just fell apart."

"He blames me for what happened because I pushed him to have a playdate with the kids here. I didn't even think about Ace, the dog we rescued, until they were almost here. I put him up in the bedroom so the kids wouldn't see him. Then they heard him and saw him when I took him out. Kids can't resist petting a dog, but his back leg is broken and in a cast."

"He was protecting himself," Nash says. "The dog thought the kids may hurt him, and he was already hurt."

"Yes."

"I'm not calling F-Phillip a dog, but I think he was hurt tonight and lashed out at you too, but he didn't really mean it."

"Whether or not he's mad at me doesn't matter if he can't have visitation with his son and daughter."

"Don't they have some sort of custody agreement with visitation and child support all laid out?"

"No. Lawyers are expensive, so they've just handled everything between the three of them."

"First things first, I think we need to get him a lawyer," Nash suggests.

"That's a good idea, but…"

"I'll pay for it," he says. "It's the least I can do for him and for you."

"Thank you," I tell him with a smile and give him another quick hug. "Having a brother is starting to come in pretty handy."

"Yeah, having a sister who is a nurse was pretty convenient for me and the MC too," Nash jokes. "Don't worry, Joanna. We'll figure out a way to make things right not just with Phillip's kids but with you and him."

"You really think we will?" I ask.

"Yeah, we will. I promise," Nash says, and I really want to believe he'll make it happen.

CHAPTER TWENTY-THREE

Joanna

"So, what can I help you with today?" Lauren Carmichael, the first civil attorney in the area who could give us an appointment, asks.

Nash, Devlin, and I are sitting across from her at the long conference table in her office, hoping we can figure out a way to help Phillip.

"We have a friend who has two children," Nash starts. "He's been paying child support without any sort of agreement with the two mothers. They only let him see the children for one supervised hour a week, and he gives them each about five-hundred dollars a week."

"Okay. So, this meeting is to talk about your friend?" she asks in confusion.

"Yes," Nash answers.

"And why isn't he here?" Attorney Carmichael asks.

"We don't want to get his hopes up," I speak up and tell her. "I'm his...was his girlfriend," I say since Phillip made it pretty clear that we're over. "And these are his two good friends. Devlin works with Phillip, so he can tell you that a thousand dollars a week is nearly everything the men make at their construction job."

"That's right," Devlin says with a shake of his head. "Honestly, I'm not sure how Fiasco, I mean, Phillip, is getting by if he's giving the two mothers all of his weekly income."

"He's barely getting by," I inform them. "He lives in a rundown apartment and barely has anything to eat. But neither of those things matter to him. He would rather spend the money to take care of his son and daughter. That's how much he cares about them, so much that he makes sacrifices for himself," I explain while blinking away tears. I will not cry while sitting here in the attorney's office. I've done enough of that the last few days, pretty much every time I think about Phillip.

"We're here to see if you can help him," Nash tells the attorney. "If you can, then I want to pay your fees for him."

"I want to help too," Devlin says.

"Me too."

"I'm not sure if I've ever seen a case quite like this before," Carmichael tells us. "If you can get me paystubs for the past two or three months, then we can figure out what a reasonable child support payment should look like. It's not supposed to be ninety percent of a father's earnings."

"Phillip gives more like ninety-nine percent," I tell her.

"You're serious?" she asks me.

"I am."

The attorney frowns and then asks, "What's brought you to my office today, though? Why are you suddenly concerned enough for your friend and boyfriend to intervene?"

"Well, that's my fault really," I start to explain.

"No, it's not," Nash interrupts. "You have to stop blaming yourself."

I explain the entire situation with Ace and Asher to the attorney, who looks less and less confident.

"The dog bite is probably going to be used against Phillip in court to try and keep him from having custody," she informs us.

"That's what I figured," I say, swallowing down the burning in my throat from unshed tears.

"We need to get the two mothers on good terms with Phillip again if you want to go forward. Could you try and talk to them? Get them to sign an agreement I draw up?"

"What will the statement say?" Nash asks.

"That they will continue to receive child support if and only if it's a court-approved custody agreement. Most mothers don't have a problem signing it because they need the financial support. Do you think these women are desperate enough to sign an agreement?"

"Yes, most likely," I say since I've seen where they live and know that they both work to make ends meet. "I'm guessing that they've come to depend on the income from Phillip. In fact, when he was recently injured and missed work, they started to refuse to let him see the children the hour on Sunday because he wasn't able to give them enough money for those weeks."

"Then let's hope they'll take our offer," Carmichael replies as she jots down some notes on her yellow legal pad. "Before I can draw up an agreement, I'll need the mothers' full names, addresses, the children's full names, dates of birth, and birth certificates would be preferable."

My shoulders slump in defeat because I know getting all of that will take time and I remember that Phillip's name won't be on the birth certificates.

"My girlfriend can help get the documents together," Nash says, reminding me about what he's mentioned about Lucy, that she's really good at finding anything you need online.

"Great," Carmichael says with a smile.

"Will it be an issue that Phillip isn't named as the father on the birth certificates?" I ask quietly.

"Are you kidding me?" she says as her face falls. "Has he even had a DNA test?"

"I asked the same question. The mothers said that he has, but I haven't seen them myself or talked to Phillip about them."

Nash clears his throat. "Lucy may be able to locate those too."

"You think so?" I look at him in surprise.

"Possibly."

"I seriously doubt that anyone can get access to those tests except for the parties directly involved," the attorney says. "They're not public record."

We all nod as if that makes a difference when we know that, with Lucy's ability, she'll probably be able to locate them.

"This sounds like it may be an even more complicated case than I first thought," Carmichael informs us. "I'll need a five-thousand-dollar retainer paid up front to bill against at my hourly rate of three-hundred dollars an hour and for any expenses incurred. Once I have those documents, I'll draw up the agreement and send it to anyone who needs to see it if you'll provide my assistant with your email addresses."

"Okay," Nash says as we all start to stand up. "I'll start getting all the documents together while Dev works on getting copies of Phillip's paystubs from work."

"And I'll sit around and twiddle my thumbs waiting, I guess," I mutter.

"We'll try to get this all done as soon as possible," Nash assures me with a smile.

CHAPTER TWENTY-FOUR

Fiasco

"Everyone is here, so let's call this meeting to order," Malcolm says from the head of the Dirty Aces meeting table before slamming his gavel down. "So, what's new?"

I don't really hear much of what's said after that. Nash starts talking about money coming in from the businesses, Dev asks if us enforcers are needed for anything, Wirth brags about how well the chop shop is doing, and Silas, well, he doesn't say much, like usual, but unlike me, I doubt he's drowning in his own head.

It's been almost a week since I last saw Joanna. Neither Giselle nor Katrina will answer the door or my calls. I left them both messages telling them I had put their money in their mailboxes on Sunday, so hopefully they got it. And even though I went to the playground Sunday at two o'clock, neither of them showed up with the kids.

I sat there for hours waiting, hoping they were just running late while watching all the other happy families play. That shit was even

133

more depressing, because the one hour a week I had was the closest I'll ever get to having a real family, and now it's gone.

A hand waves up and down in front of my face, and then I hear my name. Well, my nickname.

"Fiasco, you with us?" Malcolm asks.

"What do you want?" I ask. "Are there any assholes who need a beatdown? I wouldn't mind busting my knuckles up today."

"No, we don't have any enforcer work right now," Devlin responds.

"That's too bad. It would feel good to hit something."

"Hitting shit doesn't solve anything," Silas says.

"No, but it makes me feel less…less like this," I tell him since I don't know how to explain what's going on inside my head. It's like I've lost all hope. All the good shit that was in my life is gone.

"Things are going to get better, Phillip," Nash says from his end of the table with Malcolm. It takes me a second to realize he used my actual name. I had avoided looking at him directly until now because he reminds me of Joanna. Add to that him calling me Phillip, and it's almost too much.

"My name's Fiasco," I tell him. "Don't call me anything else."

"Joanna said you preferred to be called Phillip," he says.

My teeth grind together at just the mention of her name. "Well, I don't anymore," I grumble.

"Too bad, because I don't think of you as Fiasco anymore," Nash says with a shrug.

"I'm warning you, man, if you use my real name again, I'll kick your ass."

"You're not going to kick anyone's ass for using the name you were given when you came into this world," Malcolm huffs. "We get that you're hurting, brother. Tell us what we can do to help."

"There's nothing any of you can do."

"Are you sure about that?" Nash asks.

I glare at him for not dropping it, but at least he didn't call me Phillip.

"Yeah, I'm sure. Everything is fucked up beyond repair, just like usual for me."

"If you say so," Malcolm replies with a sigh. Then, they all finally leave me the hell alone.

~

Joanna

"THANK you both for meeting me here," I tell the women when I walk up to them with the manilla folder in my hand. They're both seated on the same bench at the playground. I look to the swings and see Asher pushing Sierra, being a good big brother. "I know you both are busy, and I appreciate you making time to talk on a Wednesday night."

"It's not like your message gave us much choice," Katrina complains. I left voicemails for both women, telling them that unless they showed up and signed paperwork, they won't be getting any more financial help from Phillip. That's not exactly true since I know Phillip and I doubt anything would stop him from helping them. They don't know that we broke up yet, though. Hopefully that works in my favor for this bluff.

"How did you get our cell phone numbers?" Giselle asks, not quite as bitchy as Katrina, but more curious than anything.

"A friend of the MC is good with finding things online," I say with a smile.

"So, what's this about signing something?" Katrina asks.

"I know that you both have been handling things…casually with Phillip until now because he's been dependable. You trust him. And you should. He's a good man. But, it hasn't been fair what you're doing to him, barely giving him a chance to see his children even though he gives you all he has for them."

"You and he lost that chance when you let that goddamn dog bite my son!" Katrina yells.

"The dog had an injured leg and Asher touched it before we could stop him. Yes, he bit him, but he didn't even break the skin. No parent can prevent every accident from happening. Has Asher ever fallen and gotten hurt while you were watching him, Katrina? What about you, Giselle? Has Sierra ever scraped her legs even though you were right there with her?"

Neither woman answers, but their lowered eyes are answer enough. "All kids get hurt at some time or another. And yes, as parents, you do everything you can to prevent as many of those events from happening as possible, but you're not psychic. I think you can both admit that Phillip loves Asher and Sierra and that he would give his life to keep them safe. I don't just mean that figuratively. I think he would honestly jump in front of a car or take a bullet to save them, because that's how much he loves them. He may not have much experience with children, but he's a great protector, and that's a pretty good start."

"What are you getting at here, Joanna?" Giselle asks.

"A civil attorney has been hired on Phillip's behalf. He would let you take the shirt off his back for those kids before he would walk away, even if you never let him see them again. I'm begging you to review this document, talk to your own attorney, if you think it's necessary, but then sign the agreement rather than take advantage of his kind heart."

I open the folder and pull out a copy to hand to each of them. "This agreement states that Phillip will continue to provide you each with forty percent of his weekly earnings. But in return, he gets one full day and the option of a night with both kids once a week on the condition that he's never alone with them. Another adult will always be there too, not because Phillip isn't capable of handling the children on his own, but because anyone could use a little help with two young kids. All of Phillip's MC brothers have volunteered to take turns until both of you along with Phillip agree to letting him have the kids without supervision."

I give the women time to read the multi-page document and watch the children play. When they're done, I add, "You'll notice that this document, once signed by all parties, also holds Phillip to providing child support; and if he ever fails to do that for more than two weeks, you'll be able to take him to court. So, it's protecting you both too."

Giselle sighs and says, "I'll have to read it over a little more at home and think about it, Joanna."

"I understand. What about you, Katrina?"

"Do we really have a choice?" she asks with a scowl.

"No, you don't, not if you want to keep draining Phillip of every cent he makes. We've added up the figures with the attorney. Did you know that he's currently giving you both about ninety-five percent of what he makes? He's been incredibly generous to the point that he's hurting himself. But now he needs a break. Let him keep twenty percent for himself and see the kids a full day each week. I know it can't be easy on him to think he may not get to see them again."

"You make it sound like you haven't talked to him about it," Giselle remarks.

"I haven't. We sort of broke up." I start to blurt out that he doesn't even know that his friends and I have been talking to an attorney for him, but that could be all the women need to tear up the agreement and walk away.

"I'm sorry to hear that," Giselle says. "He seemed to really care about you."

"Yeah, he did," I agree. "But after the dog bit Asher..."

"That's why he left you?" Katrina asks.

"Yes."

"Oh." If I didn't know any better, I would say that she looks and sounds almost sad about that. "So why are you still here trying to help him if he dumped you?"

"Because I want him to be happy, even if I'm not in his life."

"That's really sweet of you," Giselle says. "And I think we all over-reacted about the dog bite."

"Easy for you to say, it wasn't your kid that had teeth marks in his hand!" Katrina scoffs.

"Give it up, Trina! Are the marks still there?" Giselle asks the other woman.

"No."

"Then it's over and done. Joanna is right. I've been holding Sierra's hand when she suddenly trips and falls over the air and tears up her knees. They're kids, shit happens, like when Asher tried to eat that detergent pod…"

"I was in the shower, and he was only three!" Katrina shouts defensively.

"And thankfully you got out and stopped him right when he popped it in his mouth, or he could've been really sick."

"But he wasn't."

"And the dog didn't tear his hand off either, so let it go, Trina."

Katrina gets up in a huff and goes to round up Asher. He's clearly not happy about leaving the playground so soon, but he takes his mother's hand and starts to the parking lot. When he sees me, he smiles and waves his other hand happily.

"She'll sign the agreement," Giselle says as we watch them leave. "She's gotten too dependent on Fi-, I mean, Phillip's money not to."

"I hope so," I say with a sigh as I watch Katrina help Asher into his booster seat in the back of her car. I hear a pen click and look back down at Giselle. She's signing her name on the agreement.

"You don't have to rush into this. Go home and think about it and decide if you want to consult an attorney."

"I know it's a good deal, so there's no point wasting money on a lawyer," she says when she hands the document back to me. "Tell the attorney to have Phillip call me to schedule what day he wants Sierra to come over."

"Thank you," I tell her with a smile as a tear escapes the corner of my eye. "He'll be so happy to see her."

CHAPTER TWENTY-FIVE

Fiasco

"What's with the Sunday morning meeting?" I ask in annoyance when I drag my ass to the pool hall at nine a.m. on my day off.

The truth is, all I've been doing lately is sleeping when I'm not working. A few shots, and then I'm out like a light with no dreams of Joanna or playing with the kids. It's just darkness.

"We've got important shit to discuss," Malcolm says from the doorway of the chapel. "Get your ass in here. Everyone's waiting."

I shuffle my feet to the table and collapse into my chair, surprised to find everyone else looking so...awake and happy. But the difference between them and me is that they all woke up in bed this morning with the woman of their dreams next to them.

Malcolm passes out a stack of papers to each of us, sliding mine down the table.

"What's this?" I ask him.

"Read it."

I wait for someone to make a joke about whether or not I can actually read, but everyone's head is bowed, reviewing the papers.

My eyes skim over it, and I see my name in all caps, my real name. "Seriously, what the fuck is this about?"

"It's a custody and child support agreement between you and your baby mamas," Nash informs me.

"I don't understand. I fucked up when Asher got bit by the dog. Katrina and Giselle said I would never see the kids again."

"That wasn't your fault, Joanna's, or the dog's," Malcolm says. "Shit happens. Honey shoves peas up her nose every time we have them because she can. Kids will be kids, man. Our job is to just try and keep them safe from themselves, but we can't control the rest of the world."

"But what if the next thing that happens is even worse?" I ask.

"You're right. Something worse could happen to your kids," Malcolm agrees. "It sucks, but that paranoia and worry is called being a good fucking father."

After that explanation, I shut up and start reading because it seems too good to be true. Maybe I should pinch myself to make sure this isn't some sort of bizarre dream. But nope, on the last page of each of the two agreements is Giselle and Katrina's signature. They've agreed to let me see Asher and Sierra one day a week for as long as I want, even overnight; and in exchange, it says I'll pay them both forty percent of my wages.

"How much is forty percent of what we make?" I ask Devlin.

"About four-hundred dollars," he answers. "So, it's less than what you've been busting your ass to give them."

"How the fuck do you know that?" I ask.

"Because Joanna told us," Nash replies.

"Why have you...never mind," I say after remembering that she's his sister and he can talk to her whenever the hell he wants.

"Joanna not only helped us find the attorney, but she also convinced the two women to sign the agreement," Nash tells me.

"Why the hell would she do that?" I ask.

"Isn't it obvious?"

"Did you forget who you're talking to?" I huff. "No, dickhead, it's not obvious."

Some of the guys chuckle at that and then look back down at the paperwork. "What? Why is everyone here to talk about my business?"

"Because part of the agreement is that one of us will be with you when you have your kids over," Malcolm says, which is a huge relief. He holds up his hand and says, "Not because you need supervision, but I know how hard it is to keep up with one little rug rat. Two of them can get into a lot of trouble together."

"You all would really do that?" I ask.

"Absolutely," Nash agrees. "Unless you would rather have Joanna there with you?"

For a second, I think fuck yes, but then reality hits me and I shake my head. "No, she's too good for me. It would never work between us."

"Hell, man," Silas starts. "Cora is way too good for me. Same for all these other assholes and their old ladies."

"Is that true?" I ask the other men at the table. "Do you think your woman is too good for you?"

"Yes," they all agree.

"Told you so," Silas says. "That's just called getting lucky, motherfucker."

Everyone laughs at that and even I smile.

"Now that you've got your kids back, what's your plan to get your girl back?" Nash asks me.

"I have no fucking idea."

"Then we'll help you figure it out, because Joanna misses you like crazy, for some strange reason," he says with a grin.

CHAPTER TWENTY-SIX

Joanna

There's a knock on my front door when I'm sorting laundry on the bed Sunday morning, and then Ace starts barking before he takes off to the living room, making me break into a smile.

He's been moving better and better each day as he gets used to one of his legs being in a cast. I wish Phillip could see how well he's doing.

The thought makes me sad as I throw a robe over my pajamas and walk to the door to unlock it and open it.

"Phillip!" I exclaim in surprise when I see him on the other side of the glass, holding a colorful bouquet of flowers. He looks good, better than good in his usual leather cut and jeans with a white tee underneath.

"Can I come in?" he asks, making me realize that I've been staring at him for a long time.

"Oh, yeah, sure," I agree. "Get back, Ace, you know him," I tell the dog before I unlock the glass door to let Phillip in.

"Hey, buddy." He squats down to rub his head, and Ace gives his hand a happy lick. "You look like you're feeling better."

"He is," I agree.

"Good. Oh, these are for you," he says, offering me the flowers as the door shuts behind him.

"They're beautiful," I reply with a smile as I bring them up to my nose to smell them. It's a mixture of hot pink roses, orange lilies, yellow sunflowers, and some little purple flower I've never seen before. "Thank you, Phillip."

"No, I came to thank you, for all the shit that you did with the attorney and with Giselle and, by some miracle, even Katrina." He shakes his head and adds, "I'm not sure how you did it or why, but I'm really glad you did."

"Oh, Phillip. It was the least I could do. I'm so sorry about what happened with Asher and Ace."

"It wasn't your fault or Ace's," he says, crouching down to scratch the dog's ears again. "I'm sorry you got upset, buddy. Can you forgive me for being mad at you?"

Ace licks up the side of his face, as much as he can reach.

"See, all is forgiven," I tell Phillip.

"Is it?" he asks, still rubbing the dog while looking up at me with big, brown eyes.

"Of course. Dogs don't know how to hold a grudge."

"What about with us? Is all forgiven there too?" he asks as he stands up to his usual towering height above me again.

"I really hope so," I answer softly.

"Me too," he agrees. "No one has ever made me feel the way you do, like I'm smarter, funnier and better than I ever thought I could be. I love you, Joanna, and I've missed you like crazy."

"I love you too, Phillip," I reply with a smile.

Reaching for my face, he cups half of it in his big hand. "Have I told you how much I love that you use my real name and not the fuck-up name?"

"Phillip?" I whisper.

"Yes, angel?"

"Just kiss me already."

"Yes, ma'am," he agrees with a grin before he finally leans down, and I go up on my toes to meet him halfway.

EPILOGUE

Phillip

The bar smells great when Joanna and I step inside, both of us holding hands with my children. Sierra and Asher immediately spot the old arcade machines in the corner and pull away from us, sprinting over and being welcomed immediately into the group.

I look around and spot the source of the mouth-watering scent. A long table has been set up near the bar. Two older gentlemen wearing white uniforms from a local catering company are just finishing setting up a huge spread. My MC brothers are all gathered near the bar, watching the food be set while pouring fresh drinks.

Joanna gives me a smile as I take her hand and lead her to a nearby table, where Nash is sitting with his girl Lucy. I pull out a chair for Joanna, then take a seat.

"You look good," Nash rumbles as he pours Joanna and I a beer from a large pitcher at the table. "You too, Joanna. You took good care of him, and none of us are ever going to forget the help you provided."

"She's got that healing touch," I sing off-key, "that…sexual healing."

"Oh, for fuck's sake, Phil, that's my sister," Nash snaps.

"Damn, that's right," I reply, my eyes widening while I really consider the extent of what that means, and how it effects our relationship. "So that makes us…like, brothers, doesn't it?"

"We're already brothers here, in the MC, knucklehead," Nash snorts. "But yeah, I guess it's going to be a bit different moving forward. I never thought I'd see you settle down, especially not with my long-lost sibling."

"Hell, I never thought I'd live long enough to get a chance," I tell him.

Joanna takes my hand and gives it a reassuring squeeze. "I'm hopeful that things are going to be settling down in the near future," she tells everyone at the table.

"Me too," another voice says as Malcolm sits down with his wife Naomi at the table next to ours. "We've had some issues the last couple of years, problems with other MC's. I think we're past the worst of it, though, now that shit has settled with the Irish."

"You've done a hell of a job guiding us into calmer waters," Nash remarks as he turns towards Malcolm. "Where we're at now, we can go back to focusing on our legit businesses and having fun the way we used to."

"This dinner, is this how you guys used to celebrate things?" Joanna asks.

"Well, we used to have slightly rowdier parties," Malcolm replies with a faint blush coming to his cheeks. "Now that most of us are in relationships, I'm afraid there just aren't as many women coming to see us as there used to be."

When that comment earns him a smack in the arm from his wife, Malcolm leans down to focus on the plate of barbecue in front of him. Taking the hint, I jump in to try and change the subject. "Well, I'm glad to have finally met someone like Joanna," I say. "I guess I didn't know the appeal of having someone love you as a person, not just 'love you', you know, for a few minutes at a time."

"It's different, isn't it?" Nash agrees.

I look around the crowded room, really taking it all in for the first time. This bar, my second home, used to be a smoke-hazed and booze-fueled twenty-four hours a day party. Now, it looks more like a church social. Well, if the church allowed kegs of beer, tube tops, and leather clothes.

"It really has all changed," I confirm with what sounds like wonder in my voice. "I never really knew anything about family, other than being a brother to all you guys," I add as I look up and see Silas, of all people, getting plates of food for my son and daughter. "But now that I've seen this…this community, this love, from all of the ladies you've found along with all the fun we're having with the kids…"

"Is this what you were looking for all this time?" Joanna asks me softly as she leans in to speak only to me.

"I believe it was," I smile down at her. "And to think that none of it would have been possible…not my kids, not what I've found with you…if I hadn't been shot."

"Don't do it again!" Joanna warns me with a mock frown.

"Why not?" I quip with a smile. "Taking two bullets to meet you, and all the joy that it's brought me has been the best thing I've ever had happen."

"That's always the way of it," Malcolm agrees as he leans back over towards us. "There are trials in life, sure, but if you lean on your family and make it through…"

"When we make it through together, in the end, there is always a happy ending," I finish his thought. "Together, with my brothers, and all the family we have found," I add as I stand up and raise my beer to the room. "To the Dirty Aces!" I roar. "The greatest, most dysfunctional family a man could ever hope to have!"

The End

AFTERWORD

Thank you so much for reading the Dirty Aces MC series! Fiasco will be the final story for now.
If you're looking for more hot bikers, check our our Savage Kings MC series!

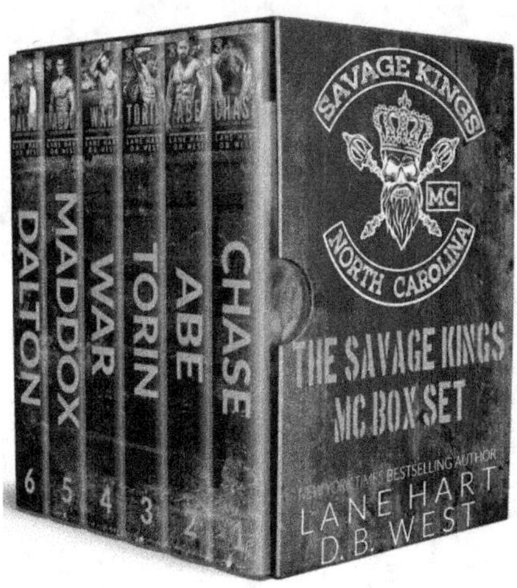

https://mybook.to/SavageKingsMCboxset

NEWSLETTER SIGN UP

Sign up for Lane and DB's newsletter to get updates on new releases and freebies!

http://bit.ly/LHDBWNewsletter

ABOUT THE AUTHORS

New York Times bestselling author Lane Hart and husband D.B. West were both born and raised in North Carolina. They still live in the south with their two daughters and enjoy spending the summers on the beach and watching football in the fall.

Connect with D.B.:
Twitter: https://twitter.com/AuthorDBWest
Facebook: https://www.facebook.com/authordbwest/
Website: http://www.dbwestbooks.com
Email: dbwestauthor@outlook.com

Connect with Lane:
Twitter: https://twitter.com/WritingfromHart
Facebook: http://www.facebook.com/lanehartbooks
Instagram: https://www.instagram.com/authorlanehart/
Website: http://www.lanehartbooks.com
Email: lane.hart@hotmail.com

Join Lane's Facebook group to read books before they're released, help choose covers, character names, and titles of books! https://www.facebook.com/groups/bookboyfriendswanted/

www.ingramcontent.com/pod-product-compliance
Lightning Source LLC
Chambersburg PA
CBHW052028150726
48002CB00002B/506